HIS RISK

A CROSSING THE LINE NOVELLA

TO TAKE

TESSA BAILEY

Entangled Publishing, LLC
2614 South Timberline Road
Suite 109
Fort Collins, CO 80525
Visit our website at www.entangledpublishing.com.

Select Suspense is an imprint of Entangled Publishing, LLC.

Edited by Heather Howland
Cover design by Heather Howland and Amber Shah
Cover art from Shutterstock

Manufactured in the United States of America

First Edition May 2013

For my father, Michael,
who taught me how to play pool.

Chapter One

Same bullshit, different city.

From the darkest corner of Quincy's bar, Troy Bennett took a long pull of his draft beer and watched men and women start to pair off, retreating to their own dark corners together. The bitter snow storm taking place outside had kept people inside well past their cut-off point. Loud music emanated from unseen speakers until everyone around him yelled to be heard or had given up and started dancing. Toward the back, a group of men played pool under an ancient light, their girlfriends looking on from the sidelines. He'd thought of joining the game himself, but since arriving an hour earlier, Troy had seen money discreetly exchange hands several times. Nothing new in a dive bar like this, but illegal gambling was something that, as a cop, he tended to avoid.

He took another pull of his beer and tried to focus on the debate taking place in front of him. His first week as a member of the NYPD had been long and tedious. Daniel and Brent, two officers who'd been gifted with the task of showing him the ropes, had dragged him to the bar to celebrate his survival.

"So let me get this straight, Danny boy. You've never once cried in front of a girl?"

Daniel heaved a breath toward the ceiling. "No, Brent. Why would I be crying if I'm *with* a girl?"

"To show her how emotionally complex you are." Brent tapped his finger against his temple. "Women go crazy for that shit."

Daniel smiled lazily in response, his attention diverted once more by the cute bartender as she passed. "When I'm with a girl, I'm a little too busy to worry about how she's gauging my emotional maturity."

In the one week since Troy's transfer from Chicago, he'd watched Daniel, the hostage negotiator, date and discard at least three different women. Brent, on the other hand, seemed more interested in blowing shit up. They were good at their jobs, and Troy considered himself fortunate Lieutenant Tyler, his former superior back in Chicago, had put in a good word for him with the NYPD Emergency Services Unit.

At the reminder of his previous home and position on the Chicago police force, Troy drained his beer and signaled the bartender for another one. He shouldn't be drinking to forget the reason he'd left Chicago, but it had become a habit of late. One he needed to get control of soon. Just not tonight.

"Weigh in on this, Troy. Do women want men who, like myself, are as deep and fathomless as the ocean?" Brent gestured to Danny with his beer. "Or pretty boy over here who hits it, quits it, and forgets it?"

Troy avoided responding right away by sipping his beer. He had a feeling his answer would inspire an entirely new debate, but he had no interest in discussing his approach to women and relationships with Daniel and Brent, who he'd known less than a week. He knew what they saw when they looked at him. Quiet, friendly guy. Passionate about his job.

It's the same thing women saw, too. In the beginning.

But Prince Charming disappeared as soon as they made it to the bedroom.

He'd tried once or twice in the past to be the guy who whispered sweet nothings into a girl's ear when she came, but he'd never been able to keep up the façade. He'd rather be explaining in very explicit terms how and where he planned to take her next. It was a part of him he couldn't explain, but had learned to embrace. Finding women to embrace it with him tended to be the difficult part.

Deciding on evasion as his best bet, Troy half smiled. "If I knew exactly what women wanted, do you think I'd be sitting here with you two?"

Both men laughed, and Brent changed the subject. Kind of. "On to more important topics, gentlemen. Blondes or brunettes?"

Daniel winked at the bartender. "You left out redheads."

Brent snorted into his beer. "I guess Danny's picked out tonight's lucky winner." He checked his watch. "Took you long enough. We've already been here a whole hour."

Troy caught a flash of something desolate pass over Daniel's face, but it disappeared just as quickly as he laughed at the joke made at his expense. "What about you, Troy? Any preference?"

He picked up his beer and tipped it to his lips. Not that he didn't appreciate their attempt at levity, but in his current mood, the hair color of a potential conquest was the furthest thing from his mind. Daniel and Brent knew the reason he'd been transferred from Chicago and thankfully, hadn't brought it up once during the week. But they were rapidly nearing the portion of the evening when he'd need to head home, since he knew too well that alcohol-plied cops didn't shy away from sensitive topics.

He had no desire for a heart-to-heart about the

circumstances of his transfer.

Dragging his attention away from the empty-bottle-strewn bar, Troy realized both men were staring at him, waiting for an answer. What had even been the question? Oh, right. Blonde or brunette.

He set his beer down, ready to deliver some half-ass answer when she walked in. His response of "both," died on his lips, to be immediately replaced with, "Her. I prefer her."

Yoga mat slung over her shoulder, she weaved her way through the bar with casual grace, observing everything but acknowledging nothing. She wore a tightly belted trench coat and jeans, remnants of the snow storm outside on her shoulders. The coat did nothing to hide the lithe body beneath, the gentle swell of her ass that begged for a man's hands. *His* hands. A long, black wave of hair obscured part of her face, but she tossed it back over her shoulder as she neared him, flashing exotic green eyes in Troy's direction, as if she'd sensed his gaze following her through the bar. That single look hit him like an uppercut to the jaw.

Brent leaned back from the bar to follow his line of sight, emitting a low whistle when he saw her. Even Daniel turned to cast an interested glance over his shoulder. A slight tightening of her mouth was the only indication that she'd heard them, but she breezed past without comment on her way to the back of the bar. After a minute, he realized Daniel and Brent were watching him, amusement blanketing their features.

"I guess we have our answer. Troy's got a thing for leggy, black-haired yoga enthusiasts."

Troy ignored them both, turning instead to follow her progress. He watched in surprise as she skirted around a group of pool players with a polite smile, then signed her name in chalk on a blackboard mounted to the wall, claiming the next game. *Ruby*. Their attention already riveted on the newcomer, the players laughed when they saw her intention was to join their obviously competitive game. She wrinkled her nose and laughed as though she was in on their joke before sauntering back toward the bar to await her turn.

She sidled up next to Troy and signaled the redhead with a dollar bill. "Hi. Can I get some quarters, please?" When the bartender turned to make change, she spoke to Troy without looking directly at him. "So, blue eyes. Why don't you stop staring and buy me a drink? I don't want to dehydrate before you work up the nerve."

Keeping his surprise well hidden, Troy studied her. He didn't want to admit how much her straightforward approach turned him on, but it did. Bad. It also made him curious, and that irked the hell out of him. He wasn't ready to feel interest, or to *care*. Not yet. No, he craved a distraction. Something, or some*one*, in whom he could lose himself for the night. He wouldn't be required to think of anything but the way she moved, sounded, felt.

Her hand rested on the bar's edge, feminine fingers curling and uncurling into her palm as if restless to touch something. He thought of that hand sliding down the front of his jeans while he sucked on her bottom lip. Her breath would catch against his mouth, right before those graceful fingers gripped him.

All at once, the idea of taking her home became irresistible. Urgent. Unable to help himself, he leaned in closer. Too close. "Ask nicely, and I'll think about it."

She stilled, the smirk vanishing from her face. Troy could practically see the wheels turning in her head. He'd shocked her right back. Good. "Now where's the fun in that?"

"I'm not particularly in the mood for fun."

"That's too bad." She accepted a handful of quarters from the bartender with a nod. "I'm a regular laugh riot."

He flicked a glance over her shoulder at the pool table. "If you're looking for fun, you won't find it there, either. I think you might be a little out of your league."

"You think so?" Amusement flashed across her face. "Care to make it interesting?"

"Bet on you to win?" Troy shook his head. "I don't gamble."

Ruby crossed her arms and leaned against the bar, facing him. "You don't gamble, and you're not in the mood for fun. Maybe I picked the wrong guy to buy me a drink. Should I ask one of your friends instead?"

Over his dead body. They weren't getting within two feet of her. "I wouldn't advise it."

"Then I'd advise you to be a little nicer."

"Now where's the fun in that?"

At having her words thrown back at her, Ruby tossed back her head and laughed. Heat flooded Troy at the sight of her long, elegant neck exposed in the soft bar light. Her lips parted to release a slow, throaty sound that he immediately wanted to hear again. "I'll tell you what..." She raised an expectant eyebrow.

"Troy Bennett."

"Troy Bennett." She repeated his name, and the muscles in his belly tightened. He had a sudden vision of her moving beneath him in the dark. Eyes closed, head thrown back as she screamed his name. "My turn is up. If I win my game, you buy me a drink. Is that fair?"

Leaning back in his chair, he nodded. "And if you lose?"

She didn't answer, merely sent him a wink and sauntered toward the pool table. After exchanging a few quick words with her opponent, who looked to be humoring her, Ruby took off her coat and threw it over a chair. Troy watched dumbfounded as she shook her yoga mat and two unconnected ends of a pool stick fell out. As she screwed the two ends together, she blew him a kiss.

Chapter Two

Ruby leaned against the wall, chalking her stick, waiting for the dickhead wearing artfully ripped jeans to break. Feeling eyes on her, she looked up and met Troy's gaze where he sat with his friends at the bar. To his credit, he hadn't turned to them the second she'd walked away to dissolve into a dude-giggle-fest over their decidedly odd encounter. Instead, he sat there watching her, all steamy and intense-like, as if he didn't want to let her out of his sight. It kind of rattled her. She liked it.

As a lifelong gambler, she'd put money on him being new in town. He hadn't quite developed that polite, polished disinterest New Yorkers tended to have. His dark brown hair hadn't been cut in a while, his clothes were a touch too casual for a Friday night. A little rough around the edges, Troy stood out.

And he'd actually refused to buy her a drink. *First time for everything.* She mentally shrugged, pushing his presence out of her head and focusing on the game.

Although Denim Dickhead had pretended to be shocked

by her offer to play for money, he'd ponied up in the end. Twenty bucks a ball. Not bad, considering it had been a slow night. Finally, he leaned across the green felt and broke. Ruby smiled as the colorful balls rolled into various positions, none of them ending up in a pocket. She began to circle the table.

All right, here we go. Mama needs a new pair of shoes. I'm taking stripes. Sink that eleven hanging over the pocket and use the rail to knock out the nine ball where it's wedged against the six. That'll leave open the twelve, fourteen, and fifteen. Once I drop the fifteen, using a little English to bring me to the other end of the table, I'll sink the nine and the thirteen into the same corner pocket, gently tapping the eight off the rail in the process so I don't get stuck later having to bank it. Knock in the ten, then I'm wide open to finish it off. I'm 160 dollars richer, and he's still a dick in ripped jeans.

Ruby leaned over the table and got to work. She tried not to let the whispers from the guy's girlfriend unnerve her as she followed her plan, methodically and precisely. It had always been her Achilles's heel. Girls her own age whispering about her. Commenting on her clothes. Wondering what kind of a girl shows up to a bar alone, late on a Friday, and proceeds to hand their boyfriend an ass-whipping on the pool table. This *kind of girl. The kind who doesn't know any other way to put food on the table.*

As she lined up her shot on the ten ball, she looked up at Troy and felt a little of her concentration slip. He didn't have an ounce of amusement on his face, like his two friends did. More than anything, he looked fascinated, like she was a puzzle he wanted to figure out.

She didn't need figuring out.

"Go ahead and order me a Maker's on the rocks. I'll be there in a second," she called to him and had the pleasure of watching his mouth tilt up at the sides. *God*, but the man was drop-dead, crazy-as-hell sexy. She'd dropped into Quincy's on a whim, never having stumbled across much competition there before, but felt lucky now that she had. If Troy turned out to be half as interesting as she suspected, she might even let him kiss her before she hopped on the R train back to Brooklyn.

As Troy turned to signal the bartender, she leaned back over the table and sunk the remaining two balls. When she finished, her opponent stood next to his girlfriend, looking, well...*hustled*. And not the least bit happy about it. Ruby tamped down a flare of apprehension when he pushed away his consoling girlfriend with a muttered obscenity and strode toward her purposefully.

"You're not getting a dime of my money," he said inches from her face. "I don't pay cheaters."

Ruby held her ground, even smiled pleasantly. "I didn't realize winning equaled cheating. It's no one's fault but your own for assuming I couldn't play because I have boobs."

His cheek twitched in warning. "You know what you need? A good—"

"Stiff drink?" Troy spoke up behind Ruby, handing her a rocks glass of bourbon over her shoulder. "That's what you were *going* to say. Right?" His words were smoothly good-natured, but she could hear the underlying steel in his tone as he addressed Angry Denim. The guy looked like he wanted to keep arguing, but when Troy silently edged around to stand in front of her, he thought better of it. Splitting a furious look between her and Troy, he tossed a wad of money on the table and walked away. Ruby slipped it quickly into her back pocket without looking at Troy.

She unscrewed her cue and replaced it inside the yoga mat, then hopped up onto one of the bar stools surrounding the pool table. Troy leaned against the high, round table, close enough that her knee brushed his stomach.

His discerning gaze swept her. "Hell of a show you put on.

How much did you make?"

Ruby sipped her drink, deciding to ignore the edge in his voice. For now. "Enough to buy groceries for the week. Pay my phone bill."

"What happens when you run into someone who doesn't appreciate being hustled and no one is there to step in?"

She set her drink down. "I appreciate your concern, but I know how to take care of myself."

"Yeah? It looked like it," he said wryly. "Who taught you how to do that?"

She pursed her lips. "You know, this is getting a little deep for a first date."

"You call this a date?"

Something her father always used to say popped into her head. *God hates a coward, Ruby.* She tossed her hair over her shoulder and met his stare head-on. "Since you bought me an alcoholic beverage and I'm planning on kissing you, then yes. I'd say this qualifies as a date."

His gaze dropped to her mouth, and she couldn't stop herself from biting her bottom lip. If the music wasn't so loud, she knew she would have heard him groan. "Sorry. I can't kiss you."

Heat suffusing her face, Ruby pushed her chair back and stood. "No kissing, no fun, no gambling. I'm starting to forget why I found you interesting."

Before she could blink, he moved to stand behind her. On either side of her, he laid his hands on the table, effectively blocking her escape. When he spoke, she felt his every word against her neck. "I just watched you bend over a pool table in those ridiculously tight jeans. Over. And over. You think I could stop at kissing?"

A shiver moved down her spine at the change in his tone. "What else did you have in mind?"

"Do you really want to know? Think very carefully before

you decide."

She swallowed with difficulty. *Interesting* didn't begin to cover this man. "Tell me."

He moved closer, his chest brushing her back. Enough to tease her, make her want to arch against him just enough to say, *the next move is yours.* His mouth hovered an inch away from her ear when he spoke. "After watching that show you just put on, I have a lot of things in mind."

One hand left the bar to brush her hip. Ruby couldn't stop herself from backing up, bringing her body flush against his.

Troy hummed, as if satisfied by her boldness. "Next time you bend over a table, I'm going to wrap all that hair around my fist and pull your head back. I want to watch your eyes glaze over when I fuck you into oblivion."

Heat shot through her entire body and settled between her thighs. She could hear her own quick intakes of breath, her accelerated heartbeat. The air she dragged into her lungs felt thick. This never happened to her. Her carefully constructed aloofness never deserted her, especially around men. But when Troy slid his hand from her hip to her belly, she shuddered under the simple contact.

"I didn't say you could touch me." Ruby forced the words out, her breath harsh to her own ears.

"Do you want me to stop?" A single finger traced the waistband of her jeans. Slowly. Invitingly.

She shuddered. "No."

"Good. Come home with me. Let me worship that beautiful body. All goddamn night."

She regained some of her composure then. What the hell was she doing? She'd stopped into Quincy's to make a quick buck and bail. Instead, she was letting this near-stranger put his hands on her. Talk to her in a way that *should* feel wrong, but didn't. At all. It felt sinfully good. Still, she didn't make a habit of going home with men she'd just met. Or engaging in casual sex. She needed to put some distance between them so she could think clearly.

Ruby pushed off the table and moved away from him, already regretting the loss of contact. "I'm not going home with you." She glanced over his shoulder where Troy's two buddies still sat at the bar, one attempting to flirt with a blonde, the other playboy-looking guy leaning back in his stool, the redheaded bartender parked between his outstretched thighs. "Why don't you follow their lead? You'd have a better chance of getting laid with someone else."

He shook his head once. "Not interested in someone else."

Frowning, she studied his features and found nothing but honesty. Where the hell had this guy come from? How could someone she'd just met make her want to break her own rules? She *wanted* to go home with him, she realized with a jolt of surprise. To see exactly what worshiping her body entailed. She'd never been so tempted in her life. It scared her a little how much. "That's too bad. I have a train to catch back to Brooklyn."

Troy scoffed. "You're not taking the subway this late. It's nearly one o'clock in the morning."

"Excuse me?" She laughed in disbelief. "I've been taking the train since I could walk."

He considered her for a moment, then shrugged. "Fine. Let's go."

She hesitated. "What do you mean 'let's'?"

"I'll ride with you to make sure the enemy you just made doesn't follow you home to take his money back. Then I'll walk you to your door and leave."

No way. Couldn't let it happen. She didn't want him to see where she lived. Not that she felt ashamed, exactly, of her microscopic studio apartment located above the Chinese take-out place.

"Your concern is touching, but I don't need an escort." He looked nowhere close to budging. "Fine, I'll just take a cab."

"You won't get a cab in this snow storm."

"You know the city pretty well for being new in town."

He regarded her curiously. "How did you know I was new in town? I didn't tell you that."

"Lucky guess."

Troy was silent for a moment, contemplating her. "There's an easy solution to this. You stay at my place. I take the couch. I'll drive you home myself in the morning, when I haven't been drinking."

She could probably lose him if she wanted to. Weave through the crowded bar, duck out the door, and shortcut down a side street before he even got his coat on. It's what she would do under most circumstances. Another part of her, however, wanted to appease her curiosity. To see where he lived, to find out what made him tick. She didn't want to say good night just yet.

And at the end of the day, she'd always loved a good gamble.

"Let me see your wallet."

His head jerked back. "What?"

"Let me look through your wallet," she repeated. "Then I'll decide if I can trust you enough to stay with you tonight."

Troy barked a laugh. "I just watched you fleece a guy for a chunk of cash and you want me to voluntarily hand you my wallet?"

"How can I trust you if you can't trust me?" They were both still a moment, eyeballing each other in the middle of the rowdy bar. Finally, with an expression that said he couldn't believe his own decision, he reached into his back pocket and tossed his wallet onto the table. She stared down in shock at the black leather wallet clipped to a shiny NYPD badge. "You're a *cop*?"

"Detective, yes."

"Now I *know* I can't trust you."

"Explain that logic."

She gestured to the pool table where a new game had started. "You just watched me fleece a guy, as you put it, and did nothing to stop me."

"I'm not on the clock."

Ruby narrowed her eyes. Damn, she usually had the ability to pick out cops from a mile away. How he'd managed to slip under her radar, she couldn't fathom. She reached down and picked up the wallet, weighing it in her hands for a moment before she flipped it open. The first thing that caught her eye was a picture of an older couple, presumably his parents. A point in his favor. They looked happy, the older man who shared Troy's good looks, and the much shorter merry-looking woman he had his arm thrown around. Pushing aside a flash of melancholy, she moved on. Gym membership, credit card, condom. She flashed him a look. He shrugged. No pictures of any kids or wifey-looking chicks. No frequent buyer card for a massage parlor. No Post-it reminders to chop up and eat anyone. He appeared to check out.

Ruby was nearing the end of her inspection when another picture grabbed her attention. Troy standing next to a man, about the same age, both wearing police uniforms. Wrigley Field towered behind them in the background. Abruptly, the wallet was snatched from her hands.

"Finished?"

She looked at him curiously. "Who is that?"

With jerky motions, he yanked his coat off the back of his chair and pulled it on around his broad shoulders. Ruby followed suit with her own coat, watching him as she did so. Something about the picture had struck a nerve. In seconds, his demeanor had gone from teasing to rigid.

"My ex-partner, Grant," he explained finally. "Did I pass

muster? Can we go now?"

She'd always been too curious for her own good. "Why *ex*-partner? What happened?" As the words left her mouth, she realized what was coming and immediately wanted to take back her question.

Troy sighed, pinning her with a look. "He's dead. Shot during a raid earlier this year."

"I'm sorry," she whispered before he'd even finished his explanation. Her stomach felt hollow. She wanted to rewind the last minute and start fresh, make him smile again. An odd reaction to have over someone she'd just met, but there it was. Damn her nosiness. With a shaky swallow, she reached over and took his hand. "Let's go."

With a curt nod in his friends' direction, he led her from the bar.

Chapter Three

Troy watched Ruby move around his half-unpacked kitchen, her inquisitive gaze lighting on every surface, taking stock of the slightest details. His take-out menus, the brand of his whiskey. He doubted anything escaped her attention. She would have made a hell of an investigator, he thought wryly. Each time he spoke, Troy could actually see her weighing his words, searching for another meaning, discerning his tone. Street smarts were probably a necessity for someone who made their living hustling people out of money. The thought made him frown.

She took off her coat and hung it on the back of his dining room chair, once again revealing those long, jean-encased legs and low-cut black sweater. He'd nearly imploded earlier, watching her bend over in those jeans. Seeing the smooth skin of her lower back peek out just over the top each time. His mind had gone wild with the fantasy of unbuttoning those jeans, wrenching them down over her ass, and hauling her back onto his waiting erection. It had been the sweetest kind of torture, sitting aroused in the overcrowded bar, hoping for a glimpse of her cleavage, while at the same time, battling the urge to belt her back into her coat so no one else had the privilege of seeing her high, deliciously rounded breasts.

The way she'd so casually and efficiently divested the guy out of his money earlier still blew his mind. Oh, she'd done it before. Many, many times. Troy had watched her opponent get progressively angry as the game wore on and luckily he'd been there to intervene. Surely she wasn't always so fortunate. He had a hard time believing the men she beat simply handed over their money once they realized they'd been conned.

He thought of the types of places she probably frequented looking for a game and inwardly cringed. A girl who looked like her caused a stir merely by walking down the street, let alone in male-dominated pool halls. What she did on a regular basis couldn't be considered safe by any stretch of the imagination.

She said she could take care of herself. To an extent, he believed her. But someone had introduced her to the world of gambling and he wanted to know who. It didn't take a seasoned detective to see she was sharply intelligent and could probably do anything she wished with her life. Yet someone had encouraged her to become a professional liar instead. One who, as far as he knew, worked alone in a dangerous city with no one to step in if things went south. It made him uneasy just thinking about the possibilities. In his line of work, he knew all too well how quickly things could go to shit. The way they had with Grant.

As always, the thought of his ex-partner sent a feeling of discomfort hurtling through his chest. He'd been presented with too many reminders tonight. First, watching Daniel and Brent interact in a way that reminded him of all too much of Grant's antics. Then again when Ruby stumbled on the picture in his wallet. But he couldn't think about it yet. The pain of that fatal night months ago still felt fresh as though it had taken place yesterday.

He looked up to find Ruby watching him closely, as if she could read every single thought in his head. Strangely, it comforted him, knowing he didn't have to say the words out loud.

"Are you hungry?"

Ruby quirked a dark brow at his sudden question. "You're going to cook for me at one in the morning?"

"Have a seat," he directed. After a moment of hesitation during which Troy suspected she was battling the urge to ignore his instruction, she pulled out a dining chair and sat, watching him expectantly. "Omelet, okay?"

"Let's see what you got, Chicago boy," she responded, her lips edging up into a smile.

Troy threw an exasperated glance at her as he walked to the refrigerator to begin pulling out ingredients. "What tipped you off? The accent?"

Her smile dimmed a little, and he remembered. In the picture she'd seen of him and Grant in their uniforms, Wrigley Field had been in the background. Thankfully, she changed the subject. "What part of town are you from?"

"Oak Park. It's a suburb just west of Chicago. You familiar?"

"I've been through Chicago once or twice," she hedged.

"Really." He pulled a Tupperware container out of the fridge and set it next to the carton of eggs. "Why do I get the feeling you weren't there to catch a Cubs game?"

She ignored his question. "Are those prechopped peppers in that Tupperware container?"

Troy cracked an egg into a bowl. "Yeah."

"I'm not sleeping with you."

"Jesus," he choked out. "How did we arrive here from prechopped peppers?"

Ruby pushed back her chair and stood, the poster child

for nervous energy. "You must cook for girls pretty often to chop up peppers in advance, that's all I'm saying. So if there are strings attached to that omelet, I don't want it. No matter how good it tastes, the answer is no."

"Actually, the peppers are for me." He gestured with the spatula. "My mother is a chef back in Chicago. It's just something she always kept in the fridge, and I guess I got used to it."

"Huh." She sat back down and watched him cook the omelet. Once he'd finished, he slid it onto a plate and set it in front of her, then pulled out his own chair and sat.

"Who taught you how to play pool like that?"

The fork paused halfway to her mouth. "I see. You cooked for me, so now I'm obligated to answer your questions." When Troy simply waited, she sighed, muttering something about cops under her breath. "My father."

"And he approves of you going to these places on your own? Using the skill he taught you to take people's money?"

"Approves?" She quickly swallowed her bite. "He encourages it."

Troy's hand flexed on the table as that infuriating piece of information sunk in. "That's great. He knowingly sends you into dangerous situations. Sounds like he really cares about you."

Ruby flinched a little at his sharply delivered words, and Troy desperately wished he could take them back. Her hand came to rest limply beside her plate, like he'd made her lose her appetite. When she spoke, her voice sounded different. Less confident. And it sliced through him. "Maybe you're right. But I don't think he sees it like that." She set her fork down, crossed her arms over her middle. "You've heard that proverb, teach a man to fish and you'll feed him his entire life? Teaching me how to play pool was his way of feeding me for life. He didn't, *doesn't*, know any other way."

Troy leaned forward. "Listen, I didn't mean to say your father doesn't care about you. I'm sorry if that's how it sounded. I just don't think hustling pool is the safest way to make money."

Her chin came up, filling him with relief that he hadn't completely shaken her self-assurance. "I didn't come here for a lecture. We just met. You have no say in what I choose to do."

"What *did* you come here for? You thought about taking off back at the bar. Searching for the quickest exit route. Why didn't you blow me off?"

She smiled a little. "You're one of the smart ones, aren't you?"

"Yeah. I am." Troy took her plate and rinsed it in the sink, then turned toward the bedroom. "I'll go grab you something to sleep in and get myself set up on the couch."

He could feel the weight of her suspicious gaze on his back as he walked down the hallway.

Chapter Four

What in the hell am I doing here?

Ruby slipped Troy's navy blue police department shirt over her head and stared at her reflection in the bathroom mirror. No one could accuse her of being a scrupulous virgin, but she didn't go home with strange men she'd known less than an hour. Ever. Especially a *cop*, for Christ's sake. What would her father, who'd taught her how to identify, avoid, and evade the police, think about her standing in a cop's bathroom, wearing department-issued paraphernalia? He'd probably never recover from his fit of laughter. As a lifelong gambler who'd introduced his only child to the lifestyle, Jim Elliott had never spoken about members of the police force with anything but disdain. She'd grown up believing they were the ones trying to keep money out of their hands and thus, food off their table.

So why was she standing there, hoping the bathroom door would open? Hoping Troy would stride inside and kiss the breath out of her. See right through her protests and take her to bed like she wanted. She didn't understand it. The relentless tug in her belly. The urge to fit her ass against his lap, wiggle her hips a little. Entice him into touching her. She'd been assailed by images of them together since they'd left the bar. He'd put the first one in her head. Bent over the pool table with her hair wrapped around his fist. From there they'd spread like wildfire.

How come the hesitation to indulge herself, then? She knew why. Troy didn't strike her as one-night-stand material. Unlike her, he came from a good family. A prechopped pepper kind of family. His eyes held a trace of sadness, she suspected over the death of his partner. Even when he laughed, it still lurked there, a reminder of his pain. She shouldn't care so much. Or be so curious to learn more about him. She should have already scratched the itch and slipped out the door as soon as he fell asleep. Only the thought of doing so left her cold. And dammit, if she left without looking back, she wasn't so sure it would be easy to forget the drink-denying, omelet-cooking, blue-eyed detective.

She pushed the troubling thoughts aside and focused on the now. Since when did she do anything besides live in the moment? Later. She would worry about the stupid feelings knocking around inside her chest later. Hell, they'd probably cease to exist as soon as she managed to work Troy out of her system.

God hates a coward, Ruby.

With a steadying breath, she reached for the hem of the borrowed shirt and drew it up over her head, tossing it on top of a nearby clothes hamper. She took a final look at herself in the mirror, naked except for her silky blue underwear, and opened the bathroom door. Troy stood in the kitchen with his back to her, cleaning the pan he'd used to make her omelet. For a moment, she simply watched him perform the domestic chore, enjoying the sight of his forearm muscles flexing as he dried a plate. Marveling over how masculine he made it look.

Troy's shoulders bunched, as if he'd sensed her standing there. As if he knew exactly what he would find once he turned around. She shivered in apprehension, resisting the urge to run back into the bathroom and lock the door. Troy tossed the pan onto the counter with a clatter and turned. When his hot gaze landed on her mostly naked body, he sucked in a breath. She forced herself to stand still, keep her hands from covering her breasts like they were tempted to do. Let him look his fill. Finally, when she thought she might catch fire under his heated gaze, he stalked toward her.

Troy kept coming until he'd forced her back up against the hallway wall. His arms shot out to rest on either side of her head, his gaze burning a path from her breasts down to her bare legs and back up again. Her skin felt bathed in fire everywhere he looked. Her nipples puckered for his attention. Goose bumps broke out along her arms. She couldn't take it a second longer.

"Are you going to spend all night looking? Or are you actually going to do something about it?"

He took another step closer, bringing their bodies flush, growling deep in his throat at the contact. She watched as a transformation took place in him. Gone was the man concerned for her safety who'd cooked her an omelet. He'd been replaced by someone raw and assertive. The change should have intimidated her, but she couldn't deny feeling a rush of excitement. Anticipation. "You might get away with running that smart mouth to other people. But you won't get away with it here. If you continue to challenge me with every word out of your mouth, I will fuck you repeatedly until you learn to play nice."

Part of her screamed in offense, the other half wanted to beg him to do it. In this moment, with a thousand sensations pouring through her, the latter half won hands down. "You'd better get started, then."

"You're going to regret that."

His mouth descended, hard and punishing, on hers. Her desperate moan collided with his as he forced her lips open and licked into her mouth. Ruby immediately went light-headed, her balance deserting her. She clutched the front of his shirt to ground herself, give herself the leverage to return his kiss, but his mouth dominated hers, rebuking her for challenging him. She fought back, pulling him closer to suck his tongue, bite at his lips. He sunk his hands into her hair, tugging just enough to let her know how close to the edge she'd pushed him. Finally, he pulled away for breath, air racing in and out past his lips.

When he spoke, his voice sounded raw. "What changed your mind?"

"Does it matter?"

"Yes." He leaned in and nipped the underside of her jaw. "It damn well matters."

Heat pooled between her legs, stealing even more of her breath. She couldn't think of anything but the truth. "Maybe I just decided to live in the moment."

Troy pulled back to study her, scrutinizing her expression. Base hunger clouding his features, he shook his head once. "No."

"What do you mean 'no'?"

Using his teeth, he scraped a path up the side of her neck. "I mean, when I sink my cock between those insane thighs, I need to know you're not going to regret it afterward." He palmed her roughly through her panties. "I need you right there with me, loving every second of me riding you. Knowing I'm going to do it all over again within the hour."

She bit back a moan as he applied pressure right where she needed it. "You're turning me down? It doesn't feel like it."

"I'm not capable of turning you down," he said on a

pained laugh, gaze devouring her breasts. "I'm going to take you to my bed and pleasure the fuck out of you. But the panties stay on. It's nonnegotiable."

Her entire system rebelled against his words. How could he touch her, kiss her like this, and refuse to take it all the way? It didn't make sense. Men didn't have that kind of willpower, did they? *She* certainly didn't have that kind of willpower. "W-what? Is it too late to give a different answer about why I changed my mind?"

"Yes. But don't worry, baby." Before she could register his intention, he'd swung her up into his arms. "Even with your panties on, it'll still be the best sex of your life."

He laid her down on the bed of his darkened bedroom, illuminated only by the light filtering in from the kitchen. His body came down on hers, pressing her into the mattress as their mouths met in a heated exchange of seeking tongues and matching groans. Desperate to feel his hard chest against her breasts, she reached down and curled her fingers in his T-shirt, then dragged it upward between them. Troy broke the kiss long enough for her to pull it over his head. Even in the dim light, she could see the tight muscles of his arms and stomach, flexing as he held himself off her. She had the sudden urge to lick every one of those muscles.

Her thoughts must have shown on her face, because Troy made a hungry noise. "Like what you see? Good. You're going to be seeing a lot of it."

He edged down, sliding lower on her body until he found her breast with his mouth. As he took her nipple between his lips, he shuddered as if drugged by the taste of her. Ruby whimpered, gripping his hair with her fingers to encourage him. He suckled her until the rosy peak stiffened, then pulled back to flick it with his tongue, watching her expression.

"Every man watching you tonight wanted your tits in his mouth." He moved across her chest to give a long lick of her other nipple. "But they're in *mine. My* mouth. Aren't they?"

"*Yes*." Her answer ended on a moan when he sucked her between his lips. Ruby could feel every movement of his mouth deep in her belly and lower. She grew increasingly damp with each tug of his mouth on her breasts and couldn't stop herself from parting her legs, sliding them up to cradle his hips. The feel of denim scraping along the soft skin of her inner thighs felt incredibly erotic, and she wanted to feel it everywhere. She rolled her body beneath him, silently asking for more.

"Tell me what you want."

"You know what I want." She nipped his jaw. "Don't make me beg for it."

He laughed under his breath. "Oh, that's exactly what I'm going to do." Breaking her hold, Troy crawled down her body until he knelt between her thighs. Strong hands gripped her knees, squeezing as if in anticipation. "Show me how far you can spread them."

She propped herself up on her elbows. "What?"

"I'm not going to ask twice." His expression was one of challenge. In the short time he'd known her, he already had her pegged, didn't he? She'd never walked away from a challenge in her life. Ruby let her legs fall open until they nearly reached the mattress on either side. She felt a surge of gratification when his gaze dropped to her still-hidden core and his breath roughened. With a knowing tilt of his lips, he ran his knuckles over the silky underwear, up and down, shifting the material over her achy, sensitive flesh. Her back arched on the pillows, and she whimpered.

"Soon, there won't be any barrier between us, Ruby. Just skin on skin. It's going to be so fucking sweet. But tonight I'm going to make you regret saying no."

"Who said no?" She shook her head once. "Not me."

Laughter rumbled in his chest. "You said no matter

how good the omelet tastes, the answer is no." One knuckle pressed and held firm against her clitoris. "Next time, maybe you'll say yes."

Then he bent down and ran his tongue up the center of her panties, leaving damp silk in its wake. Ruby dug her fingers into the comforter, her teeth clamping down on her bottom lip. Troy eased back and huffed a single, hot breath over the wet fabric, making a pleased noise in his throat when she trembled in response. When his head dipped down once more, Ruby ceased to think, could only feel as he kissed her through the silk, using tongue, teeth, and lips. She writhed on the bed, her hips bucking and twisting in an attempt to get closer to his pleasure-giving mouth.

"Is this the kind of kiss you wanted?"

How he could pummel her senses without even making direct contact, she didn't know. Didn't care. But apparently, he hadn't even gotten started. Once he'd thoroughly soaked her underwear, he stiffened his tongue and began torturing her throbbing clitoris with tight, concentrated circles. Ruby shouted something unintelligible at the ceiling, but he didn't cease his skilled torture. The hands resting on her knees pushed even wider, opening her for his hungry mouth. It felt as though the damp silk had disappeared, leaving only his tongue against her skin, even though she knew the barrier remained. Every single one of her nerve endings were firing, her thighs quaking on the bed. She tried to tighten them around his head, but he wouldn't allow it, keeping them open wide with firm hands while his mouth worked her. Ruby's release crashed through her like a hot, molten wave, burying her underneath a crushing awareness of her body. Conscious thought fled her mind, leaving her only the capability to feel.

"*Troy*," her voice shuddered out. "Oh my God."

He growled against her navel. "Goddammit, Ruby. I'm not happy that I didn't get to taste the first orgasm I milked out of you. Do you know what that means?"

"What?"

He dropped his hands to the button of his jeans, flicked it open with ease. The zipper came next. "It means I'm not done. It means you're about to be even more sorry." One hand disappeared inside his jeans. Breath hissing through his teeth, he freed his massive erection. Ruby's lips parted on a gasp at the sight of him gripping himself in a tight fist. Her body responded immediately, writhing on the bed. Just moments before, she'd felt completely fulfilled, but now she felt a powerful, driving need to take him inside her body. Her tongue licked out to wet her lips.

She reached down and hooked her fingers in the waistband of her panties, attempting to draw them down her legs. Before she could make any progress, he stayed her hand with his free one, shaking his head. "They stay on."

"You can't be serious," she cried. "I want you. I'm begging, okay? Is that what you want?"

He wedged his big body between her thighs, making her gasp when his hardness pressed against her soaked center. "Yes. Beg me to fuck you."

Ruby's breath shuddered in and out. She tightened her legs around his waist and bowed her back in an age-old method of temptation. "Fuck me, Troy. *Please.*"

Troy brought his hard body down on hers, grinding his hips against her. He swooped down to swallow her moan with his mouth, pumping his hips into her at a punishing pace. "What would you do for it?"

"Right now?" She panted. "Anything. *Anything.*"

"Would you bend over a pool table for it?"

"Yes!"

Troy altered his angle, so each forward push of his hips placed pressure right over her swollen nub, the wet, silky friction once more sailing her toward incredible pleasure.

He leaned down and scraped his teeth along the skin of her flushed neck. "Would you get on your knees for it? Take me into that smart little mouth of yours?"

Another blinding orgasm within reach, she rolled her hips frantically, working her fevered core against his thick erection. "Yes. I would. *I would.*"

Without breaking his devastating rhythm, he shook his head. "No."

A frustrated sob broke from her lips. "Why are you doing this to me?"

"What am I doing, baby?" He hooked his arms under her knees and pushed them up and back toward her shoulders, opening her for his continued assault. "Making you come?" With a final push of his hips, Ruby spiraled into another release, legs and stomach vibrating as it mowed through her. Troy dipped his head to bite the inside of her thigh, unbelievably prolonging her tremors longer than she thought possible. Struggling to find purchase, she sunk her fingers into his hair and pulled him toward her mouth for a long, hot kiss. He returned it hungrily, sucking at her tongue with a growl.

Without breaking their kiss, Troy grabbed her hand and brought it down between their sweat-slicked bodies. He wrapped her fingers around his straining erection as far as they could go and pumped into her fist. "Stroke me. *Now*, Ruby. Tight and fast. And remember that's how I like it for next time."

She didn't think. Simply obeyed. Her hand worked him how he wanted it, loving the weight of him, his gruff moans against her ear on the pillow. Knowing he'd gotten to that deeply aroused state by looking at her body, touching it, made her desperate to fulfill his needs. The feel of his barely leashed restraint in her hand sent a rush of power through her. She felt consumed with the need to give him the same pleasure he'd given her. He swelled in her hand. His hips bucked into her fist wildly.

"I'm going to come on your panties. And the next time I see them, I'm going to rip them off with my fucking teeth. Is that clear?" Her breathy reply was lost in his groan of completion as he finished in her fist. She could feel the heat of his release on that part of her still shielded by blue silk and closed her eyes to revel in the decadence of it. She'd done that to him. Driven him to this point. As much as she didn't want to admit it, the fact that he'd maintained his self-control the entire time turned her on even more. This man wasn't typical, in any sense of the word.

Possibly, he'd been right in waiting to go any further. Because tomorrow, inevitably, she would look back on tonight and regret letting him order her around, arouse her to the point that she'd begged. But right now, she felt depleted. A foreign sense of contentment that should have alarmed her, but she couldn't find the strength to battle with. She felt… conquered. If she'd stopped to ponder an hour ago whether or not she'd enjoy being dominated in bed, she would have laughed until her ribs ached. Now? If she had a tiny, white flag in her hand, she would be waving it in the air in surrender.

Troy rose from the bed and walked to his chest of drawers. He pulled a pair of black boxer briefs from the top drawer and handed them to her, watching her warily for some type of reaction to what they had just done, before turning his back. She shimmied out of her underwear and slipped on his, glad for the warmth they provided. After a minute, he climbed into bed and pulled her back against his chest to plant a kiss on her shoulder. Ruby automatically stiffened at the tender gesture.

He laughed under his breath. "Now you're shy? What happened to the girl who walked out of my bathroom naked?" When Ruby didn't answer, Troy sighed. "Sleep now, hustler. You can go back to being your difficult self in the morning. I'll even let you run your mouth as much as you need to. All day long. But when the time comes where I take you to bed, that's when I put a stop to it. Can you live with that?"

"I'll tell you in the morning," she whispered, grateful for the darkness.

"Fine. Good night, Ruby."

"'Night."

Chapter Five

Troy pulled his collar up to block the cold wind as he ducked into the police station, cursing under his breath. God help anyone who got in his way today. His mood could only be described as black, and it would still be a vast understatement. He'd woken this morning to an empty bed. No sign of Ruby. Not a trace of their crazy-hot night together. No note. Nothing.

As a law-enforcement professional and a light sleeper in general, the fact that she'd managed to sneak out on him, over countless creaky floorboards thanks to the ancientness of his apartment building, irritated the shit out of him. Infinitely more irritating than that, however, was the fact that she'd left at all. He didn't need her reassurance that they'd set the sheets on fire. They had. And he'd been more than ready for a repeat performance this morning, without the panties to get in his way. But she'd been long gone, her side of the bed barely slept in.

One worry in particular ate at him, burning a hole in his chest. Had he misread her enjoyment and pushed too far? Been too forceful? His usual need to take control in bed had been compounded by her challenging attitude. Her penchant for putting herself in danger had heightened his need to dictate her actions in the only way he could. With his body. He hadn't been able to help himself. Add in her unrestrained response to his touch, the mewling noises coming from her throat, and he'd been lost. It had taken every ounce of his discipline not to shove aside the silk between her legs and sink deep enough to lose himself. Forget his pain and responsibilities. Focusing on only *her* would have been so easy.

Another reason he'd held back.

If she'd been a different woman he'd brought home from the bar, one who didn't inspire the same possessive instincts in him, he would have had no problem removing the tiny patch of silk barring his entry. But he'd brought home Ruby the skeptic. Ruby the untrusting. She'd made him want to earn her confidence, exercise his self-discipline, and prove he was worthy of it. His restraint had been rewarded by her pulling a disappearing act, making him wonder why he'd bothered in the first place.

Luckily, Ruby wasn't the only one who made a habit of looking through people's wallets. When she'd gone to the bathroom to change into his shirt last night, he'd flipped open her wallet to find a student identification card for Baruch College in Manhattan, which had surprised him. As he'd suspected, there was much more to the sexy pool hustler than met the eye. He intended to find out just how much more. She wouldn't walk away from him quite so easily.

Troy turned the corner leading to his desk on a brisk heel, nodding curtly at a passing Emergency Services member he'd met last week. Wisely, the man didn't try to engage him in conversation. He pulled open the door of the main command area, which housed several desks and offices occupied by higher-ranking officers. The usually noisy room felt still, quieter than usual. Normally, loud phone conversations took place, interspersed with the occasional insult or ribbing of another officer. As Emergency Services occupied this part of the station, he was surprised to see detectives and officers from other departments huddled around various desks, talking rapidly.

Brent appeared to his right, holding a cup of coffee. His usual, easy smile had been replaced by a grim expression.

"What's going on?"

"One of our ESU guys was found beaten last night. Adam Tenney. Not sure if you've met him." Troy gave a single, curt nod of his head. "Guy's in a freaking coma. He's got a wife. Kids. We're trying to figure out what the hell happened."

Brent's words hit way too close to home for Troy's comfort. "Jesus."

"Yeah."

He cleared his suddenly dry throat, trying to maintain focus. "Did he put somebody away that was recently released?"

Brent shrugged one shoulder. "We just heard the news, so everyone is still scrambling. I'm sure they're going to send us all out in different directions any minute now, so be ready to roll."

"I'm ready."

Brent walked away then, leaving Troy stewing in silence. He didn't know the injured detective very well, but it didn't matter. The situation felt too familiar. Involuntary images of Grant's wife and kids crying at his funeral months earlier flashed through his mind. His chest constricted painfully. He was saved from his dark thoughts when Lieutenant Rhodes called his name from across the station, gesturing for him to enter his office. Pushing aside the fog of his memories, Troy headed in and took a seat.

Rhodes took no time getting to the point, a trait that reminded him of his former lieutenant, Derek Tyler, back in Chicago. "Listen, Bennett. You came with a glowing recommendation from Chicago. They said you weren't afraid to get your hands dirty."

"That's right." At least, he hadn't been at one time. His first few years on the force, he'd quickly gained a reputation for being fearless when pursuing criminals, without sacrificing careful planning and execution. Having found a daredevil in his partner, Grant, they'd gained the respect of their colleagues and moved up through the ranks, being placed on an elite detective squad focused on regulating the gang wars taking place in Chicago's worst neighborhoods. They'd jumped in head first, never backing away from a single dangerous situation. Troy always provided the plan and kept Grant reigned in as much as possible. They'd balanced each other perfectly. Until the night it all came crashing down.

"Good. I've got a lead I need you to run down." The lieutenant blew out a heavy breath. "I received an anonymous tip claiming Officer Tenney had gotten into some financial trouble, possibly taken a loan from a man named Lenny Driscol. If you'd been in New York a little longer, you would have heard about Driscol by now. A real jack-of-all-trades type. Loansharking, bookmaking, you name it. I thought Tenney would've known better."

Troy absorbed the information. "You want me to question Driscol. You think he's responsible for Tenney ending up in the hospital?"

"I don't *want* to think that, believe me. But they found Tenney's body in the Brooklyn Navy Yards early this morning, right at the edge of Driscol's turf. It can't be a coincidence." He gestured down to the case file open on his desk. "It's probable that Driscol didn't realize Tenney is a badge. Tenney would've kept his identity hidden."

"That only increases the probability that Driscol had something to do with it." Troy stood up from his seat. "Where can I find him?"

• • •

Ruby gathered her notebook and pens as the professor wrapped up his lecture. Around her, fellow students followed suit, eager to escape the confines of the windowless room after the two-hour class. Even she, who normally soaked up every word and took detailed notes, felt restless and edgy. As she had for the previous two days since leaving Troy sleeping in bed.

She'd woken with a jolt around four o'clock in the morning, momentarily forgetting why she'd fallen asleep somewhere besides her own tiny twin bed. Wondering whose arms were wrapped tightly around her. The memories had bombarded her all at once, sending a hot flush racing over her skin. Troy's mouth, his promises and commands, the things he'd made her beg for. Lying there, she'd waited for the embarrassment to come. But it hadn't. Only the desire for more. And that's when she knew she had to get out of there. She didn't recognize herself around him. Going home with a stranger, a *cop*, was unlike her in itself. Throw in the way she'd walked out of his bathroom naked and her shameful begging and you had someone she barely knew.

Ruby Elliott didn't beg.

So why did the thought of doing it all over again leave her breathless?

Over the weekend, she'd waited for the sharp longing for Troy to fade, but it only grew stronger every day she stayed away. She didn't want to anymore. As soon as she left class, she'd go find him. It wasn't as though she'd left him a way to reach *her*, so if they were going to see each other again, the ball was in her court. With Troy, that was how she wanted it. She'd relinquished too much control to him on Friday night,

37

but by leaving and reappearing at will, she hoped to take a little bit of it back. She'd check Quincy's first, maybe rake in a few bucks on the pool table while she waited. If he didn't show, maybe she'd pop by his apartment real casual-like. Pretend she'd left behind a scrunchie.

What makes you think he's still interested? Ruby gave her subconscious a mental one-finger salute. He'd implied there would be a next time more than once, right? So why were her nerves suddenly getting the best of her? Damn him for making her second-guess herself. Something she never did.

Deciding that if the worst possible outcome was rejection, she could live with it, Ruby stood and walked out of class, avoiding eye contact and conversation with the other students who stood in groups making plans to grab coffee together. At twenty-five, she was only older than them by a few years, but the chasm felt much, much wider. After high school, she'd spent the years wherein she would have attended college on the road. She'd only recently started making up for lost time.

The second she stepped outside the room, someone draped an arm across her shoulders, pulling her into their side. Reflexively, she jammed her elbow into the unknown person's stomach, hearing a satisfying *oompf* for her efforts.

"*God.* What the fuck, Ruby Tuesday?"

She reared back. "Bowen?"

His hands dropped to his knees as he tried to regain his breath, his dark blond hair sticking out from under a baseball cap. "In the flesh."

Glancing around, she lowered her voice. "What are you doing here?"

"Oh, thought I'd take a pottery class, you know, just to broaden my horizons a little." Ruby tilted her head at him skeptically as he straightened. "Why do you think I'm here? I came to see you."

"What for?"

"Damn. Thaw out a little, ice princess."

She sighed through a smile in spite of her irritation. Bowen, her childhood friend and all-around goofball, tended to deflate her anger quite easily. "I'm sorry. It's just, the last few times you've come to see me, it's been to convince me to come back to work for your father. And as I told you before, I'm not interested."

He made a sound of acknowledgment, turning his head to check out two of her female classmates. When they looked over, he winked, sending them into a fit of giggles. Bowen had that effect on the opposite sex. "I know. I know. You're on the straight and narrow now. You used to be fun, Rubik's Cube."

"Can you settle on a nickname at some point?"

"Rubella. Righteous Ruby. Barney Rube-el."

"Don't turn my name into a disease, and that last one didn't even work." She sniffed. "Righteous Ruby we can talk about." Heading toward the building exit, she gave Bowen no choice but to follow her. "So what's your father's offer this time? Let me guess, he's gotten word of a cash game in Jersey he needs me for. Why didn't he just come see me himself, as usual?"

Bowen looked uncharacteristically uncomfortable. "He's lying low at the moment. Waiting for a little trouble to pass."

She stopped him with a finger to her lips. "I don't even want to know. I'm not interested in hearing about any *trouble,* and I'm not interested in any games he wants to arrange so he can take a cut of my winnings." Ruby scrutinized his expression. "Just tell me you didn't have anything to do with it."

"I didn't." Bowen answered with grave seriousness, a shadow passing through his deep brown eyes. "Not this time."

With a nod of satisfaction, Ruby turned and kept walking, considering their conversation over.

"Look, we know you're still working around the city. I even heard you had a little trouble the other night." He called after her. "What's the difference how and where you play? At least this way I can watch your back."

Ruby stopped abruptly and turned. "Where did you hear I ran into trouble?"

Bowen gave a quick shrug. "People like to tell me things."

She breathed a curse. "Stop listening, then. I work for myself. I don't have to answer to your father anymore. Or mine, for that matter."

"Have you heard from him lately?"

"No." She looked away on a shrug. "Last I heard, he was working his way through Miami."

Bowen cupped her cheek in his hand in a platonic show of comfort. "You know, we could hop a flight down there and chill on the beach for a few weeks. Work at night. It'll be just like the old days. You make the cash, and I take care of any unwanted trouble. You can't admit that's not tempting."

She jerked her head out of his palm, but his hand only landed on her shoulder with a squeeze. "Why can't you just accept what I'm trying to do here, Bowen? I'm not going to hustle forever. I'm going to school so I don't have to anymore."

"You'd deny the women of Miami their chance to meet and fall in love with me?" He sighed when she didn't smile at his attempt at a joke. "Come on, Ruben Sandwich. This isn't you. What's your end game here? A boring-ass desk job where you answer to some jerk-off boss? How is that any different than working for us? If anything, it's worse."

"You know me better than that." Ruby had no intention of punching a clock or wearing a sensible business suit to work. Never going to happen. Her plans were quite different. She placed her hand on top of his larger one. "You know, just because he's your father doesn't mean you have no way out. You're capable of more than being his muscle, Bowen."

His Adam's apple bobbed with emotion. As he started to answer, a man behind her cleared his throat. Awareness prickled the skin of her neck. She knew who she would find if she turned around.

Bowen looked over her shoulder, his compassionate expression transforming into belligerence. "Help you, buddy?"

"Doubt it," the voice answered. "I'm here to see her."

Ruby turned to find a rigid Troy, blue eyes locked on Bowen and the hand resting on her shoulder. Just as she remembered, he really needed a haircut, his dark brown hair a little shaggy around the ears and neck. He wore a suit and tie as if he'd come straight from work, five o'clock shadow darkening his jaw. Involuntarily, she dropped her gaze to his mouth, the hollow of his neck. She wanted to press her face there, inhale his scent, knowing he would smell as edible as he looked.

She felt Bowen stiffen in response to Troy's confrontational demeanor. Bowen liked to fight. She'd seen him in countless altercations, occasionally brought on by her taking someone's money at the pool table, but she'd distanced herself from that and had no desire to witness it ever again. Although, she had a feeling Troy would probably hand Bowen his first loss.

"Who the fuck are you?" Bowen asked.

Troy took a step forward, and she barely resisted the urge to press herself against him. Suddenly, the two days she'd gone without seeing him felt so much longer. Now that he stood in front of her, she ached to touch and *be* touched. He'd come for her. Taken the time to search and find her. Something foreign, something resembling joy, bubbled in her chest.

"I'm the guy she spent Friday night with. And I'm the guy she's going to spend *tonight* with. So maybe the better question is, who the fuck are *you*?" As he leaned in to talk over her shoulder, his jacket opened just slightly, revealing the NYPD badge clipped at his waist.

Bowen's eyes bulged at the sight, and he laughed in

disbelief. "Are you fucking kidding me, Ruby? A cop? Please tell me this isn't for real."

She lifted her chin, refusing to feel even an ounce of the shame her friend was attempting to heap onto her shoulders. At one time in her life, she would have called herself a sellout. But not anymore. She might have been taught to think like a criminal, but she'd grown up and started thinking for herself. Perhaps she'd only spent a short amount of time with Troy, but he wasn't anything like the lazy, selfish cops she'd been taught to expect.

She rounded on Bowen, lowering her voice so only he would hear. "Maybe you *don't* know me anymore, Bowen. If you did, you would act like the friend you're supposed to be and support me. Stop trying to drag me back down with you." Pain flashed in his eyes, and she immediately regretted her harsh word choice. She sighed. "Bowen…"

"No, I get it," he said, holding up his hands and backing away from her and Troy. "Call me when you pull your head out of your ass."

Troy lurched forward, but she grabbed his shoulder just in time to stop him from going after her lifelong friend. "Don't make it worse. Just let him go."

"Who is he to you?"

"A friend." She cast a final glance over her shoulder. "My best friend."

Hard eyes scrutinized her face, searching for any sign of deception. "Do all your friends touch your face and get close enough to kiss you?"

She shrugged, trying to ignore her pulse spiking in response to his nearness, causing a little too much truth to slip out. "I don't have that many friends, so I wouldn't know. And I'm not sure I appreciate you coming here and running off my last one."

"No friends? But you're so friendly and outgoing," he

deadpanned.

Her lips twitched despite her mild irritation. "How did you find me?"

Troy rubbed the back of his neck. "I don't think you'd like my answer."

"Is that so?" Ruby wanted to question him further but decided it could wait. For the moment. She'd thought of the detective non-stop for days, and here he stood, ready to take her home. Simple. He wanted her, and she definitely wanted him back. *Don't overthink this.* She tugged on his jacket, edged a little closer. "Well, now that you found me, what do you plan to do with me?"

Eyes straying to her mouth, he groaned low in his throat. "I'm going to drive you home and make you very sorry for walking out on me."

She shook her head. "I didn't walk out on you."

"What do you call sneaking out before the sun comes up?"

"Punctual," she decided. "I had things to do."

"*We* had things to do."

Heat settled low in her belly. "Did we? I don't recall you making an appointment."

"Keep running that mouth, hustler," he rasped beside her ear, making her shiver. "I've been impatient to fuck you for days. If you keep taunting me, I'll have no choice but to assume you want it as rough and dirty as I can give it. And, baby?" He nipped her ear. "I saw the way your back arched and your thighs squeezed together when you heard my voice behind you. I know how bad you want it."

Breath raced in and out of her lungs, every inch of her reacting to his bluntness. Unwilling to relinquish the upper hand completely, she decided to put things back on even ground. She trailed her fingers across his belly, enjoying the way his muscles contracted beneath her touch. "Well, at least buy me dinner first."

Chapter Six

Troy and Ruby weaved their way through a pedestrian-filled sidewalk just off campus. He'd offered to take her out for a nice meal, but she'd insisted on having him try the "best pizza in the borough of Manhattan," until he'd finally relented. Although he felt a pressing need to get her home, Troy was grateful for the chance to rein himself in. When he showed up at her class, his intention had been to talk to her, ask her why she'd left. That plan had been blown sky high when he'd seen her big green eyes focused on someone who'd been acting a lot like a boyfriend. At that moment, he'd been overcome by the urge to drag her away from the bastard and take her home. Take what he'd somehow resisted taking Friday night. The memory of her beneath him and the most mind-blowing un-sex of his life had clung to him for days. Now that she stood right before him, he could think of little else but getting her back underneath him. This time without the damn panties.

She smiled over at him when he stepped aside to let an elderly woman pass, but it faded when she saw his expression. Clearly, he wasn't doing a very good job of hiding what he wanted so badly. Unless he regained some control and made an effort, she would write him off as someone only interested in her body. He'd tracked her down for more than sex.

Troy studied her as she moved with easy grace down the street, navigating through the crowds of people and traffic signals as if she could do it blind. She cupped her hands and raised them to her mouth to blow warm air inside, then rubbed them together vigorously to ward off the cold. Acting on impulse, he reached over and took her hands. He brought them to his mouth and huffed warm air onto her fingers, then pressed them flat between his bigger hands to heat them.

Ruby observed his actions warily. "It's only one more block."

He nodded. "So, tell me. What is it with New Yorkers and their smug superiority about pizza?"

"Hmm. Besides the fact that it's totally justified?" The light turned green, and she quickly pulled her hand away to cross the street. "Besides, aren't you Chicago folk equally narcissistic about your deep-dish pizza?"

"We prefer the term 'outspokenly confident,'" he quipped. "And what's not to like about deep dish? It's just more of the good stuff."

"There's no subtlety. You should always leave them wanting more."

"I can't relate to that," he said drily, slanting a look in her direction.

She ducked her head and laughed. "I thought you said your mother is a chef. She looks like she can make a good sauce. Did she ever make you pizza?"

It took him a second to remember that she'd seen the picture of his parents while going through his wallet at Quincy's. "How does someone *look* like they make good sauce?"

"You know…" Ruby shrugged. "She's bosomy."

"Bosomy?"

She made a noise of agreement. "Women who make good sauce are almost always generous upstairs. It's like a rule or something. Ask anyone."

"You thought it was a good idea to bring up my mother's bosoms *before* we ate?"

They reached the pizza shop, and she waited while he opened the door for her. "I'm right, aren't I? How is her sauce?"

He answered without hesitation. "The best in Chicago."

She slipped past him into the shop, not even bothering to hide her triumphant smile. Troy looked around at the small establishment boasting a glass counter displaying several types of pies. Behind it, a handful of workers slid pizzas in and out of an enormous stainless-steel oven. Farther down toward the back, a dozen orange, plastic booths were half occupied with a variety of people. Businessmen in suits, high school kids, even a priest. From an unseen speaker, mariachi music blared, blending all the noise together.

"Speaking of my bosomy mother, she would give me hell if she knew I'd brought a girl out for a slice of pizza on a first date."

"Ah, but it's our second date," she corrected him.

He leaned in next to her ear to inhale her scent. "No. Friday night was more like a fourth date. We sort of skipped the first three and got right to the best part, didn't we?"

"You could say that." She leaned in toward his mouth, and he barely resisted taking her earlobe between his teeth and tugging. "Does that mean we're going to wait three dates before we get back to the best part?"

"No, baby. It doesn't," he murmured, satisfied when Ruby shivered in response.

When they reached the front of the line, Ruby placed her order for a cheese slice to the aproned man behind the counter, then looked at Troy expectantly for his order, a heightened awareness of him clear in her expression.

"You choose. When I tell you it tastes like plain old pizza, I'm not going to listen to you complain that I must have chosen the wrong slice."

"He's just touchy because we were talking about his mom's bosoms," she said with a conspiratorial wink at the man in the apron. "He'll have a cheese slice, too, please. Followed by a slice of humble pie."

"As long as it's deep dish."

"Quiet. You're going to offend the pizza gods."

Troy grinned. As he paid for their meal, it occurred to him that he was actually enjoying himself. And how long had it been since he could truly say that?

· · ·

Ruby watched from across the table as Troy took his first bite of pizza. Somehow he managed to make the mundane look sensual, sinking his teeth in for a bite, ripping it off, and chewing slowly as the muscles in his throat and jaw worked. Her own slice sat forgotten on a greasy paper plate in front of her, getting colder by the second. She ran her damp palms up the thighs of her jeans and leaned forward for a sip of Sprite without taking her eyes off him.

"Well? What do you think?"

He leaned back in the creaking booth and considered her. "All right, you win. This is the Holy Grail of pizza. The sauce…"

Ruby tilted her head and smiled. "Is it better than your mother's?"

Troy gestured at her with a napkin. "You will never get me to say that out loud."

Eyebrows raised, she looked around the shop. "How

would she know?"

"I have no idea, but she would. Trust me. It would be like a pizza-shaped bat signal flashing over my parents' house."

"You better stay quiet then," she said with mock-seriousness. "What kind of signal would flash if she knew you were out with a girl you met hustling in a bar?"

Shrugging, he took a sip out of her drink, and Ruby's stomach clenched at the intimacy of that. "Honestly? She'd probably just want to know if you were Italian."

She pinched her fingers together. "A little bit. Enough to appreciate her sauce." Outwardly, she cringed at her impulsive comment. "Oh, God. I didn't mean that to sound weird. I'm not planning on trying your mother's sauce or anything." Sighing dramatically, she squeezed her eyes closed. "When I open my eyes, if you're gone, I won't hold it against you."

When she peeked open one eyelid, he sat smirking at her from across the table. After a second, he leaned forward and picked up her hand. With his thumb, he massaged small circles into her palm, and Ruby could feel the tiny movement everywhere on her body. "If my mother were here, she would say you're too skinny to leave that whole slice of pizza sitting in front of you on the table."

She swallowed with difficulty. "Maybe I'm not hungry anymore."

"You need to eat." His gaze dropped to her mouth. "You might not get another chance for a while, so take advantage now."

Ruby's senses fired, her body practically liquefying in the hard, plastic seat. Underneath the table, she teased his pant leg with her foot. "Take advantage of the pizza now so you can take advantage of *me* later?"

His lips twitched. "Are you playing footsie with me?"

Next to them, the priest cleared his throat loudly before exiting his booth and tossing his garbage in the trash with a righteous sniff in their direction.

They both ducked their heads and laughed. Biting her lip, Ruby edged her foot slightly higher, rubbing the inside of his knee. "Is footsie not cool anymore? I didn't get the memo."

"Oh, it's feeling pretty cool right about now." His expression heated. "Any way I can convince you to take that pizza to go?"

Every pulse point in her body beat loud and fast. "So impatient."

"I did warn you."

His voice had dropped significantly, its rough quality stroking her skin. Suddenly, she regretted walking so far from his car to get pizza. She wanted to be alone with him now, in a private place where he could give her what she needed. On Friday night, he'd driven her past the point of reason, demanded incredible responses from her body, made her say things that she'd been blushing about ever since. Now, she wanted it again. She wanted Troy to bring her home and… *take* her.

"You're not the only one who's been impatient." Her ankle brushed against his fly. Across from her, he tensed, as if fully prepared to drag her bodily across the table. "Get me home quick, Troy. Before we make a scene."

Chapter Seven

Troy barely remembered the walk back to the car or subsequent ride home after the pizza shop. Could hardly focus on anything other than the girl in the seat next to him. Crossing and uncrossing her legs. Wetting her lips. Looking up at him under heavy black lashes with such undisguised need on her face that he felt burned by the heat of it. He couldn't deny a feeling of triumph. She hadn't made finding her as easy as he'd thought it would be. When he'd called the Baruch registrar's office, they'd provided him a copy of her class schedule, but he'd been forced to wait for Monday and her first class of the week.

His displeasure over having to wait for three days made him edgy. Restless. Eager. And yet, some primal part of him relished the chase. Appreciated it, even. She'd run. He'd gone in pursuit, found her, and now he was bringing her home to take his reward. Adrenaline, mixed with sharp arousal, surged through him, making him crazy to touch her. See her naked. Make her moan. What would that first sweet shove inside her be like? Would she spread her legs or wrap them around him tight? How many times could he get her to scream his name?

Hands tight on the steering wheel, he tried to dampen the fire, just long enough to get her out of the car, up the elevator, and inside his apartment. It didn't work. The insistent throb in his pants made him grit his teeth. Even through the haze of lust, he recognized how unusual it was for him to feel this kind of urgency. He had a healthy sexual appetite that he indulged when his work allowed it. What he couldn't comprehend was his appetite for Ruby. Only Ruby. If any other girl had walked out on him like she'd done Saturday morning, he would've forgotten about it by the time he hit the shower. With her, however, he felt a constant, physical craving. It should alarm him, but he couldn't see past his need long enough to care or examine it further.

They pulled up outside his building, and he parked his unmarked vehicle in the closest spot he could find, about two blocks away. One thing he'd learned about Manhattan since moving here a little over a week ago? Parking was a bitch. Especially when the girl walking at your side along the sidewalk looked like she wanted to climb you like a tree. Troy yanked open the door leading to the building's lobby and pulled her inside by the hand. He punched the button for the elevator and released a tension-filled breath when the doors rolled open immediately.

As soon as the doors closed in the empty elevator, she ran her palms up underneath his jacket and scraped her nails back down, over his nipples and navel. His cock swelled so huge that it threatened to break through the zipper of his dress pants. Roughly, he took her hands and placed them over his erection, molding her fingers into a tight grip around it. Her eyelids drooped slightly, and she bit her lip.

"It's been ready for you since Saturday morning. It's going to take me hours of fucking that tight little body of yours to satisfy it. I hope you know what you're in for."

She looked up at him, bold and determined. "I'm here, aren't I?"

He growled, equally exhilarated and annoyed by the way she insisted on pushing him back. "I'm going to put you on your knees, Ruby. You're going to hate how much you love it."

The doors of the elevator opened, and he led her out. When they entered his apartment, he pulled her toward the bedroom, determined to have her in his bed where he'd lain awake, mentally pleasuring her for countless hours over the weekend. She followed behind him just as quickly. Then suddenly her hand tore from his, and she came to a dead stop. Confused, he turned to find her staring down at an open work file on his kitchen table, a glossy eight-by-ten photograph lying on top of several paper documents. He'd been reading through it before he left to go find her at school and forgotten to put it away. Something in her expression as she stared down at the photo sent a shot of dread through him. "What is it?"

When she answered, her voice sounded strangled. "Why do you have this man's picture here?"

He moved forward and gathered up the file. "It's a case I'm working on."

"Is that why I'm here?" She laughed without a trace of humor. "Oh my God, you're using me."

Her words sent alarm bells ringing in his head. "Ruby, what the hell are you talking about?"

"Now I know why you worked so hard to find me. I must have been like a present falling into your lap when I walked into Quincy's." Her voice shook as she turned toward the door. "God, is there one person in this city who doesn't need me to do their dirty work?"

Troy caught up with her before her fingers even touched the knob. He brought his hands up to circle her upper arms, holding her against his chest. She seemed too stunned over her false realization to struggle. A pit formed in his stomach.

He didn't know what her words meant, but he needed to get to the bottom of them immediately. Take that look of betrayal off her face. "Listen to me," he said against the top of her head. "I brought you here because I badly need to be with you, no other reason. Tell me what you're talking about."

"I don't believe you. I can't believe I fell for this. Do you know what kind of shitstorm you just landed me in?"

His anxiety spiked. "Fell for *what*, dammit? Explain."

She spun around and pointed at the file. "That man. Lenny Driscol. Don't tell me you don't know about his connection to me. Were you going to send me in with a wire or something? I'll never do it."

Troy fell back a step as her words landed on him like a ton of bricks. Nowhere in the database or in any of the casework he'd done had he uncovered a connection to Ruby. Lenny Driscol had his hand in the underground gambling world, but his customers were ex-convicts, local mafia. He'd never once thought Ruby's penchant for pool hustling placed her anywhere in his vicinity.

"Jesus. I didn't know." Hands on his hips, he paced away, then came right back. She still looked about two seconds from making a break for it, and he didn't want to give her room to escape. "Do you have any idea how dangerous that man is? You think I would risk sending you anywhere near him with a wire? Ruby, I don't even like the fact that he knows your name." Something else she'd said echoed through his brain. "What do you mean I've landed you in a shitstorm?"

"As if you don't know," she scoffed. "I have to hand it to you, detective. You were extremely convincing, even if sleeping with a possible informant might be considered unethical by police standards. You give a new meaning to the phrase 'dirty cop.'"

He'd had enough. Resting his arms on either side of her on the door, he leaned in close. "What shitstorm? I'm not going to ask again."

She got right in his face. "The boy I was with when you picked me up from school, Bowen, is that man's son. Bowen Driscol. Our fathers grew up together, and so did we. Lenny used to arrange cash games for me and my father. I used to work for him."

Anxiety, powerful and swift, settled over Troy. With a curse, he pushed off the door, away from her. She narrowed her eyes as if his reaction surprised her, but Troy barely processed it. The repercussions of what he'd done drilled into his skull. She didn't know it yet, but she was in far worse danger than she realized. And he'd unknowingly put her there. Without warning, scenes from the night Grant died played through his mind, reminding him of another time he'd put someone important to him in danger. He'd sworn it would never happen again, yet here he sat months later with the safety of another person on his head. His lieutenant had tasked him with putting Driscol behind bars, and today, in front of the man's son, he'd associated himself with Ruby.

"He had a hat on. That must be why I didn't recognize the son from Driscol's file." He sat heavily on a dining room chair, feeling blinded, his ears hearing only gun shots. "I need you to stay somewhere safe until this blows over."

"You're out of your mind." She laughed. "No one tells me where to go."

Troy shook his head. "You don't understand. Over the weekend, I canvased his neighborhood, questioning his associates about his location. They all know what I look like. Now his son has seen me with you. They'll put two and two together and think you're working with me." He looked up at her. Her eyes clouded over as she absorbed that piece of information. "You are in danger, and I'm going to protect you whether you like it or not."

After a moment, in which she assessed him so closely that

he felt stripped bare, she said, "You really had no idea."

"God, no." He stood, hating himself, the situation, and what he was about to say. "And if you're not already convinced, I'm about to get you as far away from me as possible."

. . .

Ruby watched as Troy scrolled through the contacts on his phone, presumably searching for someone who would come and stash her away for her own safety. She would never in a million years let him make a call that would threaten her freedom, but she took a moment to study him before she put an end to it. His face had gone pale, and he held the cell phone in a white-knuckled death grip. If he was acting, look out DeNiro, because they had a new Oscar-winner among them. Was it possible that his involvement with her was a coincidence? She'd never believed in them before, but his reaction negated her logic.

Damn but she really wanted to believe him. For one, just to reassure herself she hadn't lost her edge, letting a cop pull a fast one on her. Two, because the overwhelming attraction she felt for him hadn't dimmed for even a second when she'd thought he was using her. She considered those feelings twice as dangerous as anything Lenny would do to her. For a few minutes there, before she'd watched his face transform with dread, she'd been hurt. A deep, twisty, achy kind of hurt that she didn't recognize. And it sucked.

He thought her in danger. Was she in danger? Memories she'd buried deep, things she'd heard floated to the surface. Bowen climbing into her window late at night to sleep on her floor after his father put a beating on him. Neighborhood acquaintances going missing following rumors that they owed Lenny money.

One memory in particular stood out among the rest.

She'd been thirteen years old, sitting in the apartment she shared with her father on the night before Easter, waiting for him to come home so they could dye eggs. Hours passed until finally something possessed her to open the front door. She'd found him there unconscious, leg bent at an unnatural angle. After a brief moment of panic, she'd called an ambulance and gotten him to the hospital, but he'd never once confided in her what happened. He hadn't needed to. Months passed before they saw Lenny again, and even then, the relationship had been strained, centered on business. She'd known then who did that to her father.

She shook the disturbing memory, doing her best to focus on the present. Right now the only loose end was Bowen. Would Bowen betray her to his father? No. They had been through too much together, and she knew him better than anyone. He might not be ready to accept the truth, but he'd outgrown that lifestyle, same as she had. His father might be Lenny Driscol, but Ruby believed with her whole heart that Bowen stayed with him out of fear, not loyalty. She would be safe on that score, even if she would never convince Troy of that after witnessing Bowen's earlier behavior.

So was she in danger? No. And she'd worked too hard to distance herself from that world. She wouldn't hide. *Had* nothing to hide.

Troy put the phone to his ear, but Ruby sprang forward and took it out of his hands, pressing the end button. "No. I'm not going anywhere. Forget it."

He gritted his teeth. "Yes, you are. I fucked up, and now I'm going to fix it."

"You think I'll be safer surrounded by cops? If they actually make a connection between us, it'll only confirm the false theory that I'm working for you. I'm safer on my own."

"That's naïve, Ruby. You can't take on the world, contrary to what you might believe." He heaved a frustrated breath.

"Look, the last thing I want to do is send you away. Believe me. It hurts to be this close and not touch you. But I can't be responsible for anyone else getting hurt. Not again."

She frowned. "Again?" Troy didn't respond. She knew then where his anxiety came from. She'd suspected before that something more complex than mere sadness existed behind his grief. His words only confirmed it. "Your partner. You think you're responsible for his death?"

"Yes!" he burst out. "I am responsible. I should have had his back. He's dead because of *me*. Do you want to be next?"

His pain, the harshness of his confession, lanced through her chest. She should back off. Leave him to deal with the pain on his own. It's what she would want someone to do for her. But she couldn't. Didn't want him to have to handle it alone. Perhaps she hadn't fully believed before that they'd met purely out of coincidence, but Troy's pain, his insistence that she sever all ties with him, convinced her.

"What happened?"

Agonized eyes met hers. After a moment's hesitation, he spoke. "It happened during a raid. We got a tip that two rival gangs were meeting at a warehouse, probably to continue the war they'd been waging on each other for weeks. Grant and I entered on the ground floor, closer than anyone else on the team. They were right there in front of us, on the other side of a wall. Grant, impulsive as always, wanted to separate, come at them from both sides to make arrests." He shook his head. "He always wanted to take the risks. I was the one that held him back. Always. Except this time. The one time that counted."

Something squeezed in her chest. "You can't be responsible for Grant's actions. I learned a long time ago, you can't be responsible for anyone but yourself."

"That doesn't go very far in comforting his wife and kids," he responded sharply. "It doesn't work that way for me, either.

I can't turn off this need to protect you."

For years, she'd been sent by people who were supposed to care about her well-being into questionable situations and dodgy establishments to hustle men twice her age and size out of their money. Now this man, who'd known her only a few days, this beautifully damaged man, wanted to protect her. Even at the cost of a physical relationship between them. Ruby would be lying to herself if she said it didn't affect her. Make her feel cherished for the first time in her life.

Mind made up, Ruby came forward until she could look up into his face. He sucked in a breath, she suspected, at her unexpected nearness. She pushed his jacket off his shoulders before she went to work the buttons of his shirt. His tortured gaze followed the progress of her hands. "You're not getting rid of me. I'm the only one who decides where I stay. Right now, I'm choosing here. With you."

"No, Ruby. We can't anymore," he said gruffly. "Everything is different now. Whether you'll admit it or not, I'm responsible for you. This falls under the heading of me taking advantage."

His shirt fell to the floor and she paused to appreciate the swell of his chest, the sculpted ridges and dips of his stomach. "Then let me take advantage of *you*." Her seductive words wrung a groan from his lips, and Ruby felt an answering heat build between her legs. "What happened to the filthy-mouthed detective who wanted to get me on my knees?" Her nimble fingers removed the wallet from his front pocket and handed him the condom tucked in the front. His gaze sharpened on her face as he interpreted her meaning. She moved on to his belt buckle, feeding the leather through the metal loops. His erection pressed insistently against his fly, swelling with each breath he took. She slid her hand inside his pants and gripped his thick length, forcing him to place his hands behind him on the dining room table for support. Ruby knelt on the ground in front of him. "I don't get on my knees for anyone, Troy.

Remember that."

"Christ. Please don't—"

Ignoring his halfhearted protest, she took him in her mouth and tasted him, learning his texture. She swirled her tongue around the plump head, mimicking the way he'd tasted her nipples two nights earlier. He dug one hand into her hair on a throaty groan, hips rolling forward as if magnetized by her mouth.

"Goddammit, you little tease. Stop licking at it and take it deep. Show me how much you missed me."

The now-familiar transformation in his demeanor—from concerned boyfriend-type to dominant sex god in mere seconds—sent her stomach quaking, turning her legs to jelly. Hot and restless, anxious to experience more, she gripped him at the base of his erection and did as he asked, blocking every thought from her mind other than driving him to the same mindless state he'd driven her to in his bed. Stretching her lips to accommodate his size, she took him as deep as she could, then sucked on her way back up, pulling him with her mouth. He only allowed her to repeat it twice before reaching down and yanking her into a standing position. She was only given a brief glimpse of his determined face before he whirled her around and bent her over the kitchen table.

"You don't get on your knees for anyone." Troy sucked her neck hard enough to leave a mark and reached his hands around her front to unbutton her jeans. "Except for me. You'll get on your knees and use that smart mouth on me. Correct?"

"Correct." She shuddered, pushing her ass against his lap. Her entire body shook in anticipation of him finally being inside her. She bit her lip to stop herself from screaming at him to hurry, knowing he would find a way to make her sorry for making the demand.

"That's right. You will. Anytime I want it. Yes?"

"Yes. *Yes*."

He jerked her jeans down her legs, past her knees, and she stepped out of them. When nothing happened for long moments afterward, she turned to look at Troy questioningly, only to find to his eyes riveted on what he'd uncovered. Then she remembered. This morning, she'd eschewed her silky underwear for the black boxer briefs he'd given her Friday night.

"You're wearing my underwear."

She felt a flush creep up her neck but quickly crushed any embarrassment. "So what?"

He slid his hand down the flat of her stomach to disappear inside the briefs with painstaking slowness, as if he wanted to savor every touch of her skin. Long fingers inched closer to where she needed them to, taking much too long to get there. He cupped her in his palm, then pushed her forward with his body until the juncture of her thighs was wedged more firmly between his hand and the table.

His voice vibrated sensually near her ear. "Do you have any idea how much it turns me on, knowing something of mine has been cradling your sweet pussy all day long?" Without warning, he thrust two thick fingers inside her with just enough force to make her cry out, bring her up on her toes. He didn't move them, only held them there, high and tight inside her. Ruby's head fell forward on a moan that was equal parts frustrated and relieved. He'd finally filled her. But she needed so much more from him, and he seemed determined to take his time. "You walked around with your naughty secret all day, didn't you? Did you think of me while you sat in class wearing my underwear? Did the thought of me get you all wet, baby?" His thrust his fingers deeper. "Answer me or you'll get no more."

"Yes! I got very wet."

He rewarded her honest answer by stroking her clitoris with his thumb. "Fuck my fingers until I'm satisfied with your answers. What happens next depends on how happy they make me." With his hand still trapped between her and the table, she began pumping her hips against the solid pressure of his fingers, whimpering as his thumb continued its unyielding assault. "What did you think about in class, Ruby?" She released an impatient sob. "Answer me, or I'll remove by thumb."

"No. Please, don't." She sucked in a shaky breath, trying to divide her focus between talking and his insistent torture of her damp, needy flesh. "I thought about w-what would've happened if I'd stayed the whole night," she breathed, her words running together. "I thought about waking up... wondered what you would have done."

"Should I show you?" he growled.

"*Yes.*"

In the blink of an eye, he removed the hand between her legs and spun her around to face him. Her backside hit the surface of the table hard, and he pushed her legs open forcefully. Troy deftly rolled on the condom, and drove himself home inside her in one powerful thrust. Ruby's scream mingled with his shouted expletive. Before she'd fully registered his ample size filling her so completely, he began to move. He rolled his hips down at an angle, his swollen length making contact with her clitoris with each frantic pound into her.

When her head fell back on her shoulders, Troy sunk his fingers into her hair and tilted her head back up until she looked him square in the eye. "As long as you're with me, I don't want some punk thinking he has the right to touch your gorgeous face. If you want to be touched, you tell me where, and I'll take care of it. I'm the only one who touches you now, Ruby. *Me.*"

Ruby tried to think, reason through the pleasure, but her mind wouldn't allow it. She could only concentrate on Troy's calculated dismantling of her defenses. He guided her down with his body until her back arched on the table's surface, and then he straightened again.

"Stay right there. I want to see every inch of your body when you come. It's going to happen soon, baby. I can already feel your pussy tightening up on me." His feverish eyes were hidden almost completely by his eyelids, pleasure blanketing his sensual features as he continued to drive into her at a wild pace. Once again, he dipped his thumb between her legs to massage her in that perfect spot, sending her hurtling toward release.

"Oh God, Troy. Oh *God!*"

As she writhed and shook on the table, Troy gripped her knees and pushed them wider to accommodate him. Leaning down over her, he buried his face in her neck, his thrusts increasing in their intensity until she could feel the table scraping on the ground underneath them. He swelled larger inside of her, his groans of satisfaction getting louder and more guttural with each forceful movement of his big body. When he finally reached completion, her name was a growl against her neck before he sunk his teeth into her shoulder. She cried out, grateful for the shock of pain because it brought her back to earth. To where Troy lay on top of her, struggling to regain his breath, their bodies locked together like two puzzle pieces.

He pulled back to look at her. "Are you still here with me?"

Nodding, she reached up and cupped his cheek. "I'm here."

Relief transformed his face before he scooped her up and carried her to the bedroom. When he laid her down on his bed, she scooted under the covers. Troy climbed in beside her and pulled her up against his bare chest, sighing as their heads hit the pillows.

Ruby waited, knowing their conversation from earlier was

far from over. She didn't want to think about the ramifications of their mutual connection to Lenny Driscol or Troy trying to send her away. Simply wanted to lay there in his arms and collect her scattered thoughts. Behind her, however, she could feel tension slowly building in his hard frame and knew what would eventually come to shatter their momentary peace. So she shattered it first.

"What do you want Lenny for?"

Troy sighed. "You know I can't tell you that."

Her heart lurched. "Because you're afraid I'll clue him in?"

"No, dammit. The less you know, the safer you'll be." After a long silence, Troy continued. "At the very least, you have to let me put surveillance on you. For your own protection. I won't be able to concentrate otherwise, knowing you're out there. Vulnerable."

She turned to face him. "No. I'm sorry, but no. I appreciate you wanting to protect me, but I know these people. If they want to come find me, some unmarked vehicle won't stop them. They'll spot it a mile away, just like I would. It'll only make things worse for me in the end."

"You have an incredibly shitty image of cops."

She brushed the hair from his forehead. "Maybe I used to."

Troy turned his head to kiss her hand. "I can't budge on this. You have to meet me halfway. My preference would be to lock you in a safe house." A corner of his mouth quirked up at her look of horror, but quickly flattened. "I can't even protect you myself because I can't be seen with you."

She could feel herself giving in. It surprised her how little this one concession cost her. Normally, she would fight to get her way, but if this one thing made him safer on the job, helped him concentrate, she could suffer through it. "All right, copper. I'll make you a deal. If I spot your surveillance guy, I lose them. If they can stay well hidden, I'll let them stay."

A relieved smile transformed his face, tripling her feelings of guilt. Because in the back of her mind, she knew with absolutely certainty that she wouldn't be able to stay out of it. Starting tomorrow, he'd have her help whether he liked it or not.

Troy took both of her hands in his and rolled her over. He ripped open a new box on the nightstand and removed a condom, then slid it down his swelling erection. With one push of his hips, he seated himself deep inside her, eliciting a moan from Ruby's throat.

"See how easy that was, hustler?"

Then he leaned down and kissed her, swallowing her persistent cries with his mouth as he started to move.

Chapter Eight

Troy looked up as Daniel entered the precinct, Brent and Matt close behind. For the first time since they'd received the news about Officer Tenney being found beaten half to death in Brooklyn, they looked like they had good news. Troy certainly needed some. He'd left Ruby pretending to be asleep in his bed this morning. Knowing they needed to talk but also very aware of the fact that spending the night with him had been a concession in itself, he hadn't pushed his luck. If he pressed her too hard, forced her to promise she wouldn't take unnecessary chances with her safety, she might break their hard-won agreement about the surveillance.

Knowing she had a car following her was the only thing keeping him from losing his mind as he sat behind a desk, narrowing down Lenny Driscol's possible location.

She thought she'd kept her intentions hidden the night before, but he'd seen them in her eyes. He needed to solve this case before she found some way to interfere. The night he'd met her, he'd recognized her curious nature, and she wouldn't be happy taking a backseat for long. She would not only threaten the case, but her safety in the process. Not to mention, it had taken some fancy footwork on his behalf to convince Lieutenant Rhodes to assign the protection detail and not bring Ruby in for questioning instead. Troy didn't have long, however, before the man's patience ran thin and he started looking for information anywhere he could find it. He couldn't allow Ruby to be used as a possible source, something that could endanger her welfare, but he needed to work quickly or it would be unavoidable.

One thing he knew for certain. If he didn't stop thinking about all the possibilities of what could happen to her, he would never get anything accomplished. *Concentrate.*

His silent command helped for all of two seconds. Scenes from the night before played on an endless loop in his mind. Ruby kneeling in front of him, Ruby beneath him, Ruby's dark hair spread out on his pillow as she slept beside him. He'd woken up half certain she wouldn't be there. But she had been. She'd placed her trust in him, something he suspected she didn't do easily. Now he needed to earn it. Once a girl like Ruby gave her trust, her heart would follow. He meant to earn that, too.

Daniel propped a hip on his desk, breaking the cycle of his thoughts. "Morning, Bennett. You want the good news or the bad news first?"

"Good," Brent answered for him. "Always take the good first."

Shaking his head at Brent, Matt pulled up a chair and sat. "Tenney woke up from his coma this morning. We just got back from the hospital. No permanent damage."

A wave of relief rushed over Troy. "Great. That's great. What's the bad news?"

"Brent is still here," Daniel deadpanned.

"Funny, asshole," Brent returned, seemingly unaffected. "The bad news is that tip we received about Tenney being involved with Driscol proved out. Tenney told us from his hospital bed that one of Driscol's guys worked him over."

Troy nodded, unsurprised. He'd already been convinced that Driscol was responsible, based on the fact that he'd gone into hiding and the evasive answers he'd gotten when questioning his associates. "That gives us what we need to bring him in."

"Right. It'll take us a day to put a team together. First, we need his location."

Troy pushed his notes across his desk toward the men. "I've got it narrowed down to two places. Both in Brooklyn. Now that we know Driscol is our guy, the lieutenant will put more bodies on this. We should easily have his location by tomorrow."

Brent picked up his notes and scanned them quickly. "Heard you put surveillance on a possible witness? The lieutenant wasn't exactly forthcoming about the details."

Troy shifted uncomfortably, knowing he had to come clean. His conscience wouldn't allow him to leave his fellow officers out of the loop, unaware that a possible wildcard was in play. "Remember the girl pool player from Quincy's the other night?"

"The long-legged beauty with all that black hair?" Daniel's grin spread wider. "Sure, I remember her."

Troy glared at him, then quickly explained the connection between Ruby and Driscol.

Brent's eyebrows shot up. "Are you kidding me? She could lead us right to him."

"Not going to happen," Troy enunciated. "We're not putting her at risk. She's not one of them anymore, and if her association with me is discovered, we'll be doing just that. We find Driscol on our own." He turned to find Matt watching him silently.

"Guess a lot has happened between Friday night and this

morning."

"You could say that."

Brent's head dropped forward into his waiting hand with a *smack*. "Please don't tell me you fell for this girl. She cheats people out of money for a living." Troy didn't answer, merely raised an eyebrow. He had no interest in discussing his relationship with Ruby. Not when an axe still teetered so precariously over their heads, waiting to fall. "Thank Christ this emotional bullshit will never happen to me," Brent continued. "If I ever see it coming, I'm going to haul ass in the opposite direction like I've got ten mother-in-laws chasing me with rolling pins in their hands."

Matt gave an uncharacteristic laugh. "Your time is going to come, Brent."

"The bigger they are, the harder they fall," Daniel chimed in with a nod.

"Fuck that. If I go down, I'm taking you all with me."

Daniel sighed. "I assume you'd be taking me along for advice on pleasuring a woman? You see, there's this thing called a cl—"

"Are you lovely ladies finished?" Troy broke in impatiently. "We've got two locations to scout, and we don't have a lot of time."

• • •

Ruby walked briskly down the sidewalk, throwing occasional glances over her shoulder. Evening had fallen, and the cold wind nipped the skin of her cheeks. After hiking her yoga mat higher on her shoulder, she dug her hands into her pockets for warmth. She'd spotted the unmarked police car five minutes ago, but she had to admit they were doing a good job of staying inconspicuous. If she hadn't known to look for them, their presence might not have registered.

Too bad she was about to lose them anyway.

She'd walked for a good half hour to a billiards hall in the East Flatbush section of Brooklyn she hadn't frequented in over a year. The surrounding neighborhood had taken a turn for the better, college kids attending school in the city taking advantage of the cheaper rent in Brooklyn as opposed to Manhattan. New stores and coffee shops had popped up shortly thereafter to take advantage of the new blood. *Her* destination, however, had remained true to itself, standing out among the new developments like a sore thumb at the end of a row of empty warehouses. A broken-down eyesore, Hildebrand's Billiards hopefully still drew the same rough crowd it always had, in addition to the newer, younger crowd invading the neighborhood. In fact, Ruby was counting on it.

If she could do something to keep Troy from tangling with Lenny Driscol, she needed to do it. This was *her* dark, twisted world. She had the kind of access he would never have. And unlike every other man in her life, he hadn't tried to use her to his advantage. He truly wanted to keep her removed. Safe from harm. She knew what Lenny Driscol was capable of. Her father, who'd never been scared of another soul or a dangerous situation in his life, had lived with a healthy fear of Lenny. He'd warned her on several occasions to keep her mouth shut about anything she saw or heard pertaining to the man. Had even hinted at the possibility that Lenny might have friends on the police force or in political office who kept him out of trouble.

She couldn't sit by and watch the same fate befall Troy as it had so many before him. Her own father, even. Not when she could so something about it.

She ducked into the yoga studio she'd looked up online this afternoon after returning from Troy's apartment. A man in a white robe standing behind the counter looked up expectantly with a welcoming smile on his face. "Welcome.

Are you here for the seven o'clock class?"

Ruby ignored his question. "You have a back door in this place?" He looked confused, but obviously interpreting the urgency behind her expression, pointed toward a dimly lit studio toward the back. "Great. Thanks." She started walking in the direction he indicated but came up short, turned, and picked up a brochure off the counter. Maybe she'd come back some time and see what all the fuss over yoga was about.

A moment later, she slipped out the back door into the alley running behind the studio. Knowing she only had about an hour before her personal surveillance team realized she wasn't actually taking a yoga class, she hastened toward the back entrance of Hildebrand's.

The crack of pool balls and bass-heavy classic rock greeted her as she pushed inside, immediately noting her favorite table stood empty in the corner. She skirted around a group of college students in trucker hats drinking Pabst Blue Ribbon and made her way to the bar, grateful when she recognized the stocky man behind it. Pulling a pint with one hand, Gerard smiled wide in greeting.

"Well, shit. If it ain't Ruby Elliott. Where you been at, girl?"

"Around," she said with a mysterious wink. Out of the corner of her eye, she scanned the bar for the man she'd come to find, but didn't see him. "Mind if I knock a few balls around?"

"Go on ahead. Your table awaits." Gerard leaned forward on the bar and dropped his voice. "Just do yourself a favor and don't take any money off my new hipster clientele. They'll write a Yelp review faster than you can blink, and that ain't good for nobody."

"No worries, Gerard. Their money is safe tonight. I'm only here to practice."

He straightened once more, suspicion tightening his

mouth, but he didn't comment. Anyone who'd known Ruby a year ago wouldn't believe she would waste her time in a place like this unless there was a pile of money waiting at the end of the night. Before he changed his mind and questioned her further, she grabbed a tray of pool balls off the counter and headed toward her table.

Forty-five minutes passed without any sign of her man. Ruby tried to appear disinterested in the comings and goings of customers into Hildebrand's but felt herself beginning to get nervous. She needed to walk out the front of the yoga studio within fifteen minutes or the unmarked car would report back to Troy that she'd ditched them, which would lead to a series of questions she didn't want to answer.

Just as she was about to give up hope, she saw Tim Keith walk in through the front entrance and park himself at the farthest end of the bar. Gerard automatically began building a pint of Guinness for Tim, a Hildebrand's regular and neighborhood lifer. If information existed about Lenny Driscol's whereabouts or what he'd done to put the cops on his trail, Tim Keith would know the details. Now she had to find a way to get the lowdown without trying too hard.

Ruby re-racked her balls, shoved her stick back inside the rolled-up yoga mat, and headed toward the bar. Sliding into the seat beside Tim, she sent a smile in Gerard's direction. "Ginger ale, please?"

"You got it, honey." Ruby turned to find Tim watching her closely, so she smiled back casually. "Hey, Tim. Long time no see."

Tapping an unlit cigarette against the bar, he nodded. "Haven't seen you in this neighborhood in a while. What brings you by?"

"Just missed it, I guess."

"Huh."

Gerard set her drink down in front of her, and she took

a sip to wet her suddenly dry throat. Tim had never been anything but friendly toward her, but he now appeared mildly suspicious. She should have gotten up, cut her losses, and walked out right then, but she stayed rooted to her seat. If she wanted to help Troy, she needed information. And besides Bowen, who she definitely couldn't go to in this case, she had no other way of retrieving it. Ruby leaned back in her chair, trying to appear relaxed, and waited for him to speak.

"Haven't seen your daddy around in a while, either. Is he still working with Lenny, or is he following your lead and turning over a new leaf?"

She ignored Tim's question about her father, knowing he'd only asked it to needle her. "Actually, this new leaf I turned over isn't all it's cracked up to be. I'm thinking about asking Lenny for my old job back. I can't get the same kind of action working solo." Her cell phone went off in her pocket, and she ignored it, knowing it had to be Troy. Her time had run out. "I can't seem to find him. Any idea where he's doing business now?"

Tim's sharp eyes met hers, delved deep for any kind of deception. Her friendly, open expression didn't waver. He seemed to make a decision then, his body relaxing in the stool. Finally, he pulled out a pen from his coat pocket and scribbled an address on a napkin before sliding it across the bar in her direction. When she reached for it, he held on to the edge. "This place is just a hunch. He dropped out of sight almost a week ago, and no one really knows where he went." He lowered his voice. "He put a beating on a badge last week for some unpaid debt. Put the freaking guy in a coma. Now he's got another cop sniffing around, so he's more than a little paranoid." Tim shook his head. "I hear he's already marked this new cop as next on his list. He's starting to lose his touch for subtlety."

When Ruby slipped back into the alley moments later,

her mind ringing with Tim's words, she forgot all about walking back through the yoga studio so her tail could follow her home.

I hear he's already marked this new cop as next on his list.

She needed to work fast.

Chapter Nine

Sitting in the dark stairwell of Ruby's building, Troy tried to fight his mounting panic. He'd received a call from the surveillance officer at eight o'clock telling him Ruby had gone into a yoga studio and never come out. His guy had canvased the neighborhood with no luck. She'd been long gone. Troy, wanting to go look for her himself, had been forced to sit and wait, aware that showing his face anywhere Ruby had recently been would be a bad idea. Being in her building, even hidden inside, wasn't exactly the greatest idea he'd ever had, but the desire to see her clouded his judgment.

An hour having passed since the call, she still hadn't come home and wouldn't answer her goddamn phone. Fear mixed with irritation and helplessness. An intolerable combination in his current frame of mind.

Troy shot to his feet with an expletive, intending to go look for her when he heard the sound of a key turning in the lock. His heart felt ready to beat itself out of his chest as he waited to see who would enter. The heavy metal door pushed open to reveal Ruby, looking half-frozen with the damn yoga mat slung over her shoulder. She was beautiful, her hair floating around her shoulders courtesy of the wind gusting in through the door. In one hand, she held a half-eaten chocolate doughnut.

She'd actually stopped for a doughnut while he'd sat there, fearing for her life? With that, his anger reached its boiling point. "Where the hell have you been?"

Ruby's entire body jerked with a cut-off scream, and the doughnut fell to the floor at her feet. She backed up against the wall, searching wildly in the dark, and finally noticed Troy a second later. When she saw him standing a few feet away, she sagged with undisguised relief, one hand pressed over her heart. "Oh my God," she whispered. "Are you crazy? You almost gave me heart failure."

Regret moved in his chest. It served to deflate some of his anger, but not all. Not by a long shot. "No. *I'm* not crazy. Crazy would be blowing off professional protection to go buy a fucking doughnut."

Angrily, she kicked the fallen doughnut at him, barely missing his dress shoe. "A doughnut I only got two bites out of!"

"Don't try and be cute," he warned, shaking his head. "I am pissed as hell, Ruby."

"We had a deal," she said with a shrug, having the grace to look mildly contrite. "I spotted your guy, so I split. Next time, send someone with half a brain."

"He's the best I could find besides myself. He's former military."

"And yet…" She wrinkled her nose, head tilting to the side. "He lost me."

Troy laughed darkly. "Oh, you have no idea the kind of fire you're playing with, baby."

With an irritated huff of breath, she tried to skirt past him on the stairs. "Why don't you go cool off, then? It's my ass in trouble, so let me worry about it."

"*No*, dammit." He stopped her progress past him with a firm hand on her elbow. "Believe it or not, I care about what happens to you. The last hour has been pure hell, Ruby. You think it's funny to scare the shit of out of me?"

Her belligerent expression deserted her, and she looked away. "No. I don't think it's funny. I didn't do it to scare you."

"Then why?" he demanded.

"I…" she started hesitantly, then blew out a breath. "I needed to go make some money. I can't do what I do with a cop watching my every move."

Troy shook his head. "You don't think I briefed them on your usual activities? They weren't going to interfere unless you were in trouble." He let go of her arm. "Would it be so much to ask for you to give me a little credit?"

A long pause ensued as they both regrouped from the argument. When Ruby spoke, her voice was barely above a whisper, telling him how much the apology cost her. "I'm sorry." He nodded once in acknowledgment but didn't say anything. She moved in front of him, trying to meet his gaze, but still righteous in his anger, he stared resolutely over her head at the wall. Until she stood on her toes to kiss the underside of his jaw and the now-familiar heat settled low in his belly. "You know why I'm wearing my hair down today?" Another kiss, this time lingering on his neck. "You marked up my neck last night with that filthy mouth of yours. And you know what else?" Troy felt his defenses slipping. Against his better judgment, he looked down and immediately got lost in her green eyes. "I like it. Having your marks on me."

His cock swelled against the front of his pants, begging for the stroke of her hand. Ruby's scent, her lips tracing the column of his neck, the body he'd memorized hiding beneath her coat all threatened to topple his anger, but the memory of his fear remained too fresh. He needed to regain the control she'd wrested from him. Needed promises he knew she wouldn't give.

He grasped the wrist trailing down his chest toward his stomach. "Tell me the truth first. Were you only hustling tonight? The *truth*, Ruby."

Hesitating for the barest of seconds, she smiled up at him. "Would I lie to you?" Too late. He'd caught her hesitation, and now he had his answer. She hadn't been able to stop herself from interfering. Appeasing her boundless curiosity. Knowing her, the innocently posed question would be the closest he came to the truth tonight. It appeared that, in order to retain his sanity, he would need to regain his lost control in another way. He couldn't let her know he was on to her. Yet.

Troy brought her hand to his mouth, kissed the inside of her wrist. "Do you remember what I told you the first night I brought you home?"

She looked momentarily thrown by his sudden change in direction but answered him smoothly. "You said quite a lot that night. Narrow it down for me."

He pulled her closer. Let one hand slide down the back of her coat to squeeze her tight ass, satisfied when her breath hitched in her throat. "I told you I would tolerate your smart mouth, your goddamn evasiveness, during the day. But when it comes time to take you to bed, that's when I put an end to it. I won't allow you to hold back anything when I'm fucking you." His teeth bit into her earlobe and she whimpered. "Now do you remember?"

Warily, she nodded. "Yes."

"Good." He hitched her up against his body, forced his hips between her thighs. "Just so we're clear, baby, that's what I'm doing. Letting you divert my attention with your tempting body so you don't have to answer my questions or explain where you went tonight. I'm *aware* of it. I'm the one who's *letting* you get away with it." He gave a single upward thrust, letting her feel his need. Her eyes closed, mouth parted on a moan. "And you won't be getting away with it for long. I'm not feeling very charitable toward you at the moment."

• • •

Troy lifted her with one strong arm, and her legs automatically wrapped around his waist as if she'd been made for him. As though they'd performed this same dance a thousand times even though it felt new, exciting, arousing. His stride sure and confident, he ascended the stairs toward her apartment. Ruby tried to focus on him, kissing his neck and breathing in his scent to calm her racing heart, to no avail. She'd never met anyone who could see through her so easily. Call her so accurately on her bullshit. It made her want to trust him. Never tell him another lie. He'd only known her a matter of days and yet, knowing her background working for the criminal he was tracking, he'd trusted her enough to leave her alone in his apartment that morning. Found a way to let her retain her freedom even though she had potentially damning information to use against him. Ruby felt a desperate need to repay that trust. Troy thought she was worth more than whatever money she could earn in a single night. Time to prove it.

She'd never brought anyone into her apartment. When she'd left her father to his own devices on the road to return home, she'd finally found her own space. Unlike the drab, impersonal motel rooms she'd been frequenting, this was her home. Sharing it with something else was a big step, but it felt right. She wanted the memory of him in her bed, his scent on her pillow. To share a part of herself with him that she'd kept hidden for so long.

Troy came to a stop at her door and let her slide down his body. Feeling suddenly self-conscious, she averted her gaze to dig the keys from her pocket.

"Hey," he said, tipping her chin up, frowning when her smile trembled. "I think this is the first time I've ever seen you look nervous."

Shrugging, she tried to appear unaffected by his observation and failed. "I've never brought anyone here before. Or whatever."

Something primitive flashed across his face as he moved closer. "Except me."

"Except you," she whispered a second before his mouth locked itself to hers, draining every ounce of tension wrought by the interminably long day from her body.

Until that moment, she hadn't realized how much she'd needed him to kiss her. The last hour had left her tense, reminders of her past life making her feel exposed, like an imposter. She drew strength from the contact of his hungry lips. It made her feel whole in a way that nothing else ever had. It should've alarmed her how easily his mouth commanded her mood, but the sensations it elicited left no room for her to care.

He pulled away, keeping his gaze locked on her mouth like he couldn't contain his need for more. "Let's get inside before I peel off those jeans and take you hard against this door."

Biting her lip to refrain from begging him to do just that, Ruby turned and pushed open the door. Schooling her expression, she whispered to him. "Just keep your voice down. I don't want to wake up my husband."

Behind her, Troy tensed. "You better be joking."

Ruby threw him a wink over her shoulder and flipped on the overhead light. She turned to Troy to gauge his reaction. He scanned the room, landing on everything within seconds, eyebrows lifting in surprise. Attempting to see the apartment through his eyes, she looked at the unfinished pool sticks and spec sheets pinned to all four walls and drills, glue, and tools stored neatly on every available surface. The entire back wall was lined with finished pool cues of varying size and brightly colored wraps.

Troy carefully pulled a cue down from the holder. He turned it over in his hand, then threw an amazed glance in her direction. "You make these?"

She swallowed. "Yes."

"You make them *here*? In the apartment?" He shook his head in disbelief. "They're amazing."

Relieved for something technical to focus on, she spoke quickly. "Some of it, like the wrapping and varnishing, I do here. I rent a wood lathe at a local guy's shop for the actual carving of the maple." She shifted uncomfortably. "I'm saving up for my own lathe. They're expensive so…"

He closed the distance between them. "So you hustle."

Ruby nodded seriously. "I've already got a business model worked out. As soon as I get my degree, I'm going into business for myself. I want to do this right." She met his gaze. "I'm not going to hustle forever."

"Of course not." Cupping the sides of her face, he half smiled in a way that made her heart rate stutter. "God, don't you know how incredible you are? You can do anything you want."

A powerful feeling spread through her chest, one she didn't have a name for. He believed in her. And at that moment, she didn't need anything else. Just this man standing in front of her, looking down at her like he couldn't believe his luck at having met her. It humbled Ruby. Made her want to be as amazing as Troy seemed to believe she was capable of being. She'd revealed her dream to him, one she'd never shared with anyone, and he'd accepted it, praised it even. He didn't tell her to stick to what she knew, or stop trying to aspire to unrealistic dreams. She'd never in her life experienced that kind of unconditional support. It made her want to reveal everything about herself, to just lay all the good and bad at his feet to let him pick through the debris.

"Thank you," she said, not surprised to find her voice sounded shaky. Turning her head, she kissed his palm. "Are you up for one more adventure tonight?"

Chapter Ten

Ruby peered down at her hand, swallowed up by Troy's larger one as they walked through the alley behind her building. She hadn't revealed their destination, yet once again, he'd trusted her enough to follow her back down the stairs and out into the night. Around them, steam rose from subway vents in the concrete, televisions flickered in people's windows, and wind whipped past them in steady gusts. All familiar to her. Home. Noticing how he inspected every dark corner of the alley suspiciously, looking for any sign of trouble, she elbowed him in the ribs, smiling playfully.

"You look fully prepared for an alien attack."

He pulled her into his side protectively. "Please, for the love of God, don't tell me you walk through here alone at night. Or during the day, for that matter."

"Okay, I won't tell you that." She grinned at his warning look. "Although, it would make us even for scaring me half to death earlier."

"You deserved it," he grumbled. "I swear, you're going to give me an ulcer. I'm too young for an ulcer, Ruby."

"It's not much farther," she said. "Soon we'll be safely inside where you can scold me for my recklessness and manhandle me into promising I'll do better."

"I'm only mildly appeased."

"Mmm. We can do much better than that." When he tried to lift her off the ground into his arms, she squirmed out of his grip and jogged toward a padlocked door located along the brick wall of the alley. "Here it is." She pulled a thin, metal object from her pocket and inserted it into the lock. "Don't look now, but here comes that ulcer." With a few calculated twists of her wrist, the lock popped open. She removed it from the metal loop and opened the door, gesturing for him to follow as she walked inside.

"Jesus," he groaned, dragging a hand down his face. "A little warning would be nice before you involve me in a felony."

"And ruin the surprise?" She flipped a switch on the wall. Over their heads, a dozen lights came on, illuminating a deserted tavern. "Oh, good, they haven't cut off the power yet."

Troy circled the room, the wooden floor creaking beneath his feet. Furniture sat neatly arranged in sections, and portraits of famous Irish writers lined the walls. It felt as though moments before, it might have been filled with people. He came to a stop at the full-sized pool table located in the center of the space. "All right, what is this place we have forcibly entered without permission?"

Ruby dug a few quarters out of her jacket pocket before hanging it on the back of a high stool. "The Wheelhouse Tavern. Closed down about a month ago. It's still cleaned regularly because they've been showing it to prospective buyers." Sending him a wide smile, she rubbed her hands together. "Feels like the heat's been left on, too." She crouched down and placed the quarters in the slot of the table. The balls sped down, landing with a crash, and she began to rack. "Fancy a game?"

"What the hell." He shrugged off his jacket with a heavy sigh. "I'm already an accomplice. Might as well make it worthwhile."

"That's the spirit." Ruby stood and jiggled her ever-present yoga mat, dislodging both halves of the stick inside. Quickly, she screwed the ends together and moved around the pool table to stand in front of him, holding it out for him to take. "Your break."

Watching her suspiciously out of the corner of his eye, he took the stick. He grabbed a cube of blue chalk off the rail, quickly chalked the tip, then leaned down to line up his shot. "This isn't the stick you used the first time. That one had a burgundy wrap."

Behind him, her eyebrows shot up. "You remember that?"

"Yeah," Troy said in a low voice, sending the cue ball down the table to break the tight rack. Two solids rolled into different pockets, and he straightened. "I remember everything about you that night."

With well-hidden shock, she watched him round the table, sinking another three balls, his form and execution well beyond that of a beginner. She couldn't help the smile that tugged at her lips. "Why didn't you tell me you could play?"

He shrugged in the act of chalking his cue. "You didn't ask. Besides, there's a lot we still don't know about each other, right?"

Ruby's good mood dwindled. Obviously, despite the mild improvement in his attitude toward her, he still hadn't gotten over his earlier anger. She took a deep breath, sensing she would be revealing more about herself than she had already. In a way, she felt she owed him some honesty. "What do you want to know?"

"In what capacity did you work for Lenny Driscol?"

"Wow. Straight to the point. Don't you at least want to know my favorite color first?"

"I already know its green." He sunk another ball. "Look, you don't have to answer if you don't want. Nobody's forcing you."

There it is. The challenge. She hated that he'd played that irresistible card even as she respected it. Crossing her arms over her middle, she steeled herself for his reaction. "I guess I should start from the beginning."

Troy's head came up, a look of surprise crossing his face. He hadn't expected her to talk, Ruby guessed.

"My mother left when I was very young. So young I can't remember her." She blew out a heavy breath. "My father, Jim, has always made his living playing pool. When she left, he couldn't afford day care or a babysitter, so he took me with him. I grew up in pool halls. Even after I started going to school, they were where I spent my nights and weekends."

Troy stayed silent, listening intently from across the table, pool stick forgotten in his hand.

"We went on the road during summer vacations. Stayed in a town long enough to make some money, then moved on. Eventually, it became too much. Too many wildcards when you walk into an unfamiliar place." She saw Troy's hand tighten on the stick and decided not to elaborate on that. "We came back to Brooklyn, and my father hooked back up with Lenny. For a while, everything was great. Lenny found cash games, sent me and my father in, and we gave him a cut of the winnings. Then one time, Lenny shortchanged my father. They argued… It got ugly." She shrugged, trying to hide the hurt at being abandoned. "My father went back out on the road, and I stayed here."

"He left you," he stated angrily. "Yet you continued working for Driscol?"

Ruby nodded. "Pretty much the same gig, only Bowen

started coming with me. He stepped in if things got out of control."

"How often did that happen?" Troy's voice cracked like a whip, making Ruby flinch. She held little appreciation for the look on his face. Not judgment exactly, but something resembling incredulity at her decision making. She had the sudden urge to tell him exactly how bad it had been. To see how much truth he could handle before walking away. She held no regrets about anything in her past, and it was time he knew it. Whether or not he could accept it would be up to him.

"Often," she finally answered, her chin coming up. "The final match I ever played for Lenny ended in a brawl. Bowen has been a fighter his whole life, but even he couldn't take on the eight men who wanted a little revenge for having a girl make them look like Grade-A assholes on their turf. I barely escaped out the back door in time. Spent the night hiding in a Denny's parking lot."

Troy tossed the stick onto the table, and she watched it roll to a stop against the rail. He rounded the table in her direction, fury blanketing his expression. "Did you tell me that little story just to piss me the hell off?"

Ruby straightened her spine, resenting the excitement that flowed through her over what his intentions were. What he would do when he reached her. "Yeah. Maybe I did."

He pulled her body against his. "Well, it fucking worked." His mouth stamped over hers, cutting off her surprised gasp. Ruby couldn't resist moaning when his hands sunk into her hair, tugging her head to the side so he could slant his mouth over and over across hers. When he pulled a little harder than necessary on the long strands, she bit his bottom lip in reproof, but it only made him deepen the kiss, his tongue licking into her mouth with a possessive growl.

"Do you know why you wanted to make me angry?" He

spoke directly against her parted, panting lips. "Because you know it makes me hard. You know it makes me hot to fuck." He tilted his hips and pushed against her, demonstrating the effect of her words. "That means you're hot to *get* fucked. Good. Too bad you're about to get much more than you bargained for, hustler. Turn around."

She hesitated. Not because she didn't want to turn around, but she didn't feel like giving in to his order so easily. With an impatient noise, Troy gripped her waist and whirled her until she faced away from him. Her breath shuddered in and out, sounding loud in the empty bar, betraying her need for him. He worked the button of her jeans, then slid his big hand down the inside of her panties. Ruby's stomach and thighs tightened as if on command. She cried out as he dipped two fingers inside her, then spread the wetness in achingly slow circles around her clitoris. "You can make this a lot easier on yourself by agreeing. No more disappearing. No more dangerous situations. None of it. Agree to it, Ruby. *Now*."

Biting her lip, she shook her head. "I can't."

He pushed his long fingers inside her, high and tight, forcing her midsection against the pool table. She thought she might have called his name, but couldn't be sure. "I protect what's mine. Are you denying that you're mine, Ruby? I'd seriously advise against it."

"N-no, I'm not denying it," she panted, and was rewarded by the continued massaging where she desperately craved his touch. Her head fell forward, her palms supporting her weight on the green felt. Suddenly, the sweet pressure disappeared, and she felt her jeans and underwear being pulled roughly down her legs. Sobbing in anticipation of what was to come, she pressed back against him and circled her naked bottom against his lap. "Please, Troy. I want it."

He leaned down and spoke harshly next to her ear. "Not yet. Not even close. Congratulations, you've pushed me past my limit today. When I decide you've earned it, you'll get it fast and rough. Not a second before."

Confusion mixed with eagerness to see what he had planned. What had he meant by making her *earn it*? Without thinking, she leaned forward and placed her upper body flat along the table, putting her backside on display in front of him. He rewarded her with an uneven groan, palming her ass with his callused hands, kneading the flesh with ungentle fingers. "Does this feel good enough for you, or would you rather I make it hurt?"

Ruby's head dropped forward onto the table's surface with a whimper. The answer left her mouth before she could analyze it or change her mind. "Make it hurt."

With his right hand, Troy picked the pool cue off the table. Behind her, she could hear him unscrewing it, separating the smaller, thinner top from the thick base. Not knowing his intentions only served to heighten the anticipation. His roughened breath, his own obvious excitement, shot liquid warmth through her. A moment later, Ruby felt the cue's top half tracing over the curve of her bottom. The cool, smooth wood felt foreign and soothing moving across her fevered skin. Then, in a move she didn't anticipate, Troy brought down the thin shaft of wood in one hard swat on her ass.

She sucked in a breath and let it out with a shudder. Nerve endings snapping, pulse drumming like mad in her ears, all she could think was *again*. "More."

"There's always more, baby." He repeated the action exactly ten more times, bringing the wooden shaft down to snap against her sensitive flesh until she couldn't decide where the pain ended and the pleasure started. It became the sole focus of her entire being. Each swat elicited a moan from her throat in the form of his name. Just when it became too much, when she thought she might combust from the tornado of sensations taking place within her, he stopped. Then the smooth, glossy wood slipped between her thighs until one end rested on the table, the other in his hand.

"You found out what my limits are today, didn't you?" He skimmed his free hand up her back, then down to rest beside her hip. "Now we'll test yours."

Very slowly, Troy drew the cue back and forth, sliding the midsection of the wooden shaft against her damp flesh with perfect accuracy, angling it just enough to put pressure where needed. Ruby's legs threatened to give way beneath her, every part of her now focused on the slick friction passing between her legs. She tipped her head back and closed her eyes, imagining what an erotic image they created, Troy using her pool cue to pleasure her body. His touch, the harsh words uttered from his lips, corrupted her little by little, and she loved it. As if he was calculatedly ruining her for anyone else, any touch beside his own. He wanted to find out how much she could take. And he was using pool, the thing she loved most, to teach her a lesson.

"You like that, don't you?" Troy's voice sounded raw, sensual. "I can tell by the way you're working those fuck-me hips. You're going to work them exactly like that for me later."

"Yes," she said on a choppy breath. "I will."

All conscious thought fled as he began twisting the cue as he stroked, teasing her in a new way. With a whimper, she undulated her hips, her body hurtling toward release. Her breath came in little pants, thighs shaking, nipples tightening painfully as Troy's movements pushed her closer to the edge. Then all movement of the cue ceased, the pressure gone. Ruby cried out in protest, her head falling forward.

"Want more?"

"*Yes*. Please."

The slippery pressure returned, and once again, he used the cue to rub her past the point of reason, stopping just before she could orgasm. When he'd repeated the same torture three more times, Ruby tried to turn around, to lash out at him with her fists, but he merely pressed her against the side of the table and tossed the pool cue aside. In one, swift motion, he seated himself deep inside her, nearly toppling her forward onto the table. Ruby screamed at the unexpected filling of her body. Her muscles clenched tightly around him, shuddering as she finally came.

"I can't get into that damn head of yours," Troy growled against the back of her neck. "You're so goddamn determined to keep me out. But your body knows who it answers to. It answers to me, doesn't it?"

Ruby had only begun to recover when Troy pulled himself almost completely out of her body, then thrust home once more, pushing deep enough to bring her onto her toes. "Troy. *Troy*." She repeated his name over and over, unaware of what she was trying to say or how many times she said it.

"Let me in, Ruby," he ordered, sliding deep once more. He wrapped her hair around his fist and pulled her upright. Kissed her neck sweetly. "Let me *in*."

With a sob, Ruby's head dropped back onto his broad shoulder. "I've let you in more than I've ever done before. With *anyone*."

"It's not enough. I want it all. I need everything you have." Releasing her hair, he gripped her hips in his hands and began driving into her at a pace that stole her breath. Dizzying pressure stole through her once more as her body worked to answer the increasing demands of his. Behind her, Troy groaned as he neared his own peak, his length swelling even thicker inside her, stretching her to accommodate him. "Give it to me. Just surrender everything, baby."

His grated command, combined with the punishing fingers digging into her flesh, sent her flying. Her shaking body milked his as he released inside her with a final groan of her name. He rested his forehead in the center of her back, bathing her in harsh exhalations of his breath. Ruby's entire body felt liquefied, utterly replete, and if the table hadn't been supporting her, she would have been in a heap on the floor. Suddenly, Troy's impassioned words came back to her, bringing tears to her eyes.

Let me in. I want it all.

She hadn't even been capable of answering him. He'd begged her to open herself to him emotionally and she'd remained silent, denying them both something special, acknowledging this incredible connection between them. Years spent rebelling against being labeled a coward now seemed stupid and meaningless. She'd been one tonight. Still was. Something broke inside of her. She managed to prevent any tears from escaping, but a small sound slipped past her lips.

The mouth tracing her back stilled. "Ruby?" Troy pulled her up gently by the shoulders and turned her around to face him. He searched her face, blue eyes bright with worry, raising his warm hand to cup her cheek like she might break. "Jesus." He sucked in a breath. "Did I— Are you hurting?"

With a shake of her head, she rushed to reassure him. "No, you didn't hurt me."

He deflated in relief. "Then what is it?"

The words died in her throat. She wanted to make him promises, tell him she wouldn't take any more risks with her life. But it wouldn't be true. She still had one more thing to do. If she tried to explain her reasons to Troy, what she planned to do for him, he wouldn't understand. He'd take it as a blow to the ego, or worse, he'd find a way to detain her. She'd been brought up to believe deeds, not words, proved your worth to someone else. Perhaps that logic didn't apply here, between them. But it would always be an absolute truth in her world.

She'd come to care for him deeply in such a short space of time. His life was now in danger. She could prevent him or any more of his colleagues from getting hurt. Prevent him going through the pain of losing Grant all over again. It all seemed black and white to her, when to Troy it would be a giant mess of gray. Could she somehow make him understand without giving herself away?

"Ruby?"

"If you really want me, you need to be patient. I can't change overnight." She took a deep breath. "I know I'm a colossal pain in the ass, but try not to give up on me."

He supported her face in his hands, promises and a touch of humor in his expression. "Hey. You're *my* colossal pain in the ass. And I'm not going anywhere."

A laugh bubbled from her throat. "Okay, Troy Bennett. Then I'm going to let you spend the night. But you should know, I'm fresh out of peppers."

The corners of his mouth edged up into a smile. "Don't worry. I can be creative."

Ruby glanced down at the forgotten pool stick. "Tell me about it."

Chapter Eleven

Troy focused on the map of the Brooklyn Navy Yards spread out on the conference table in front of him, detailing the area surrounding the warehouse where they would hopefully be arresting Lenny Driscol within the hour. After days of around-the-clock stakeouts and working various informants, his lieutenant and a majority of the officers felt 100 percent certain that Driscol had been lying low in the basement of a decommissioned garment factory.

Troy didn't share their conviction. Something about it didn't feel right. They'd placed officers in the condo development across the street to surveil the warehouse for the past two days. During that time, they had seen dozens of men come and go, practically jumping around and waving a red flag that Driscol was hiding out inside. It felt way too easy. Driscol couldn't have survived this long by being stupid.

Two streets over sat another empty warehouse, the second location they'd been considering for a possible hideout. Not a single person had walked out the front door in days, so they'd made the call to rule it out. Yet the uneasiness in him remained.

He wanted it over and done with. Not only because Driscol deserved to be put away for meting out his own brand of justice and putting one of their own in a coma, but because he didn't like Ruby being so close to the situation. As long as Driscol remained on the street, Ruby would be in danger by association. Danger from Driscol. Danger from herself. Take your pick. She was hiding something from him. Troy knew it in his bones. The sooner they arrested the son of a bitch, the sooner he could breathe again.

Somehow, he'd gotten himself tangled up in the very predicament he'd faced with Grant. He'd formed an attachment, albeit a *very* different kind, to someone who played fast and loose with her own safety. Grant hadn't known the meaning of the word *caution* and neither did Ruby. He'd left Chicago to escape the constant reminders of his partner, how he'd failed to have his back when he needed it most. He couldn't fail with Ruby.

The simple act of *being* with Ruby placed her in jeopardy. She'd run with a crowd that wouldn't take kindly to their secrets being shared with law enforcement. He'd turned her into a threat to dangerous people. A possible source. He knew he should leave her in peace. Protect her by staying away. Yet he couldn't. And after their night and morning together, he didn't think he'd be capable of walking away even if he wanted to.

The multicolored map in front of him blurred together as he recalled waking up in Ruby's apartment. He'd risen early, intent on leaving before sunup so there would be no chance of being spotted at her building. But this time, the second time they'd woken up together in the same bed, she hadn't pretended to be asleep. She'd pushed him down onto his back and ridden him so hard he'd been frantic with the need to come by the time she'd finished, shuddering and moaning on top of him like something out of his most erotic fantasies. It had been another hour before he'd managed to drag himself away, and even then, he'd wanted to go back for more. Ruby knocked his socks off in jeans and a coat. But hell, naked and rumpled, her voice husky from sleep, desperate to take him inside her? She'd made him burn like crazy.

In fact, he needed to stop thinking about it right now, in a room full of officers who would definitely notice if he got a hard-on, seemingly from studying a map.

"He's in there. I know it," his lieutenant said from across the table. "We've had round-the-clock surveillance on the building since Monday. They might not have been discreet, but then again, Driscol doesn't have a discreet bone in his body. It's hard to believe he's even stayed out of sight this long. He must know he's finally screwed the pooch."

Next to him, Daniel pulled a face. "That phrase needs to be retired, like yesterday."

Brent shrugged. "I kind of like it." He held up his index finger. "Wait, did you say pooch or coo—"

The lieutenant let out a long-suffering sigh. "Can you two jackasses be serious for one minute?" They nodded. "Good. We've got to make this clean. Matt and Daniel, you're coming through the south entrance. Brent, you're with Bennett."

Troy massaged the back of his neck where a warning sensation had developed. "Lieutenant, something about this is off. We haven't scouted for back entrances at the other location because we didn't want to tip our hand, but it's possible they're entering in a different way. If we go ahead and bust the wrong warehouse and they get wind of it, Driscol will go so far underground that we'll never find him."

Brent considered him a moment before turning to the lieutenant. "He might be right, sir. It feels too easy. Maybe we should hold off until we're sure we can rule out the other location."

Troy's phone started vibrating in his pocket, disturbing his concentration. He tried to ignore the incessant buzzing because they were in the middle of a crucial discussion that he'd instigated, but when it didn't stop after two unanswered calls, he pulled out his phone to check the screen. When he saw the caller's name, his heart rate doubled. The officer he'd placed on Ruby had called three times, back-to-back.

"Lieutenant, I need to take this." He hit the answer button. "Bennett. What's going on?"

"I followed her as far as I could without getting out of the car and chasing her. The street leading to the warehouse is all blocked off for street repair," came the officer's booming voice, laced with frustration.

His mouth went dry. "What the hell are you talking about?"

"She hopped off the bus wearing a different jacket than when she'd left her apartment. Must have changed on the ride over. She turned the corner toward the warehouse before I even knew it was her."

Troy pinched the bridge of his nose, trying to think clearly over the roaring in his head. *Ruby in danger.* "Hold on. Which warehouse are you talking about? The one we're set to move on this morning doesn't have construction outside."

"I know. It's the other one." He snorted. "Just waltzed right in like she was taking a Sunday stroll. Funny, I thought you guys ruled out that location."

"We did rule it out." Every officer in the room watched him, knowing something had gone terribly wrong. Troy felt like he was being strangled. He stood in a room full of armed men wearing bulletproof vests, discussing the safest entrance strategy for the arrest of a dangerous criminal, and she'd walked right in, completely defenseless.

Troy dragged a hand down his face. "Goddammit, Ruby." He hung up the phone and turned toward his fellow officers, anxiety searing every part of his body. "We have to move. Now."

• • •

Ruby slipped in through the warehouse door being held only slightly ajar by a bald, stone-faced man with an earring that looked vaguely familiar. Of course, these protection types were almost always bald and stone faced with an earring, so that didn't mean a thing. She winked to throw him off a little. One valuable thing her father had taught her was to *brazen it out*. In situations such as these, when every move you made would be under suspicion, act like you owned the damn place. That kind of behavior tended to distract people long enough to get what you needed. Or annoy them into *giving* you what you needed if only to get rid of you faster.

Once she confirmed Lenny was indeed hiding out in the warehouse, she could call Troy with the information. He would make the arrest and get himself out of Lenny's crosshairs where he would be safe. None of his colleagues would be in any danger, either, something she suspected he worried about constantly since the loss of his partner. She could have given him the address to the warehouse last night but had quickly decided against it. She could get useful information by going in first. Information that would help ensure Troy came out on the other side alive.

She also needed to warn Bowen.

"Who are you?"

"Ah, come on. You don't remember me?" Mr. Clean showed zero reaction. "Ruby Elliott. Our kids play softball together!"

"I don't have any kids."

"Yeah, me neither." She moved farther into the dusty warehouse, quickly eyeing every possible exit. "Listen, you mind telling Lenny I'm here? I don't have a lot of time."

He grunted. "What makes you think Lenny's here?"

"A hunch." She pursed her lips. "A hunch you pretty much confirmed when you opened the door. Why else would you be standing in this abandoned warehouse in the middle of the day? I'm sure you'd much rather be updating your eHarmony profile or taking a yoga class. Incidentally, I'm thinking of taking one myself."

Recognition dawning on his face, he pointed a finger at her. "Wait a minute. I remember you. The chick pool player. Jim's kid."

Ignoring the pang in her chest at hearing her father's name, she spread her arms wide. "In the flesh."

A smile broke out across his face, making him almost handsome. Almost. "Well, come on then. He's in back."

"That's more like it," Ruby murmured under her breath, following him through the enormous, sunlit room filled with sawdust and empty crates. "You guys really need to fire your cleaning lady."

"We don't get a lot of people coming in this way," he continued jovially, divested of his suspicion. As far as he was concerned, they were cut from the same cloth. A realization that made her feel queasy. "There's an entrance through the parking garage around back we've been using." He threw a wink over his shoulder. "It's like we're not even here."

"Stealthy." Ruby pretended to let the piece of information go in one ear and out the other. "The pizza delivery guys must hate you."

Laughing, he stopped as they reached a wooden door at the back of the warehouse and nudged it open with his foot. She breezed past him into a dark hallway and continued on toward another closed door with light emanating from the edges. Her pulse began to race as she grew closer, but she refused to consider the possibility that she'd made a bad decision in coming here. She would stay long enough to confirm that Lenny was here and get as many details as she could before hightailing it back to her end of Brooklyn.

Her escort reached a hand over her shoulder to push the door open. Ruby tried not to show any outward reaction to seeing Bowen and half a dozen men sitting at a round table, reading the newspaper and smoking cigarettes. All sporting weapons. As usual, Bowen boasted a black eye and several painful-looking cuts on his face. Quickly, she counted seven other men seated around the room, pausing in their conversation to eye her with interest. Her friend's gaze widened when he saw her standing in the doorway, then flicked toward Mr. Clean, who'd gone to join them at the table. The other men looked between her to Bowen, waiting for his reaction.

Only a few seconds had passed when his chair scraped back, and he came toward her with open arms. "Ruby Doo, what's the haps?" To anyone who hadn't known Bowen since childhood, he would appear carefree, delighted to see her, but she saw the wealth of worry in his eyes. He threw his arms around her and whispered in her ear. "I didn't tell them anything, but you shouldn't be here."

"Neither should you. I'm sorry, Bowen," she whispered back. The way his body tensed, she knew he understood her reason for coming. He knew the cops were coming and that she'd come to warn him. Ruby held on tight to her faith that he wouldn't tell Lenny. That he'd see this as his way out. Maybe he'd been pulled deeper into his father's world, but he was still the same boy whose wounds she'd bandaged in back alleys and motel bathrooms. Her best friend. And he didn't belong here any more than she did.

Bowen sighed shakily against her hair then pulled back, smiling broadly once more, but she could see the conflict in his eyes. He spoke up loudly enough for everyone to hear.

"Lenny, I knew she'd change her mind. Ruby's back. Just like the old days."

She tensed as Lenny sauntered in from an adjoining room. All confidence and swagger, he nonetheless looked as though he'd had a few sleepless nights. Lenny had always been an undeniably striking man, but his dark blond hair had started graying at the temples, his age causing the skin of his cheeks to sag. He wore black dress pants and a white button-down shirt rolled up to his elbows. Intelligent eyes raked over her, lingering on her face. She didn't smile, knowing Lenny would find that suspicious. They'd never had anything but a business relationship.

"Took her long enough," Lenny finally said, his thick Brooklyn accent echoing through the room. He placed a hand on Bowen's shoulder. Besides a flicker of irritation, her friend's easy expression didn't waver. "But like I'm always telling Bowen, you don't just walk away from easy money."

Easy for who? Ruby wanted to ask, but wisely refrained. "I guess you're right. Here I am. You have a game for me or not?"

Lenny threw back his head and laughed. "You certainly haven't changed, kid."

"Yeah, well. Leopard. Spots."

He jerked his head toward her. "This girl is fearless. I think your time away from her might be the reason you're starting to go soft on me."

"I ain't going soft," Bowen said quietly.

Lenny laughed in obvious delight of having created an awkward moment, but then his smile disappeared. "You are if I say so, son." His gaze bored into hers. "And you'd be wise to learn some respect."

"Please, just give me a time and location," Ruby said, bringing the focus back to her. "As much as I'm enjoying your company, I have things to do."

The older man's eyes narrowed on her. She held her breath, praying she hadn't pushed too far. Then he reached inside his pants pocket and pulled out a notepad. Without asking, one of the men handed him a pen, and he scrawled an address. When he ripped it out and handed it to her, she feigned disinterest and shoved it into her jacket pocket. "Are we done?"

"For now."

With a nod toward Bowen and Mr. Clean, she turned and headed toward the door. Suddenly, she wanted badly for Bowen to come with her. She'd planned on doing her part and trusting him to find a way out on his own, but an uneasy feeling gripped her over the possibilities of what he might do. Her shoulder blades itched as she walked from one end of the dark hallway to the other, but she didn't turn around for fear they would see the anxiety on her face.

A minute later, Ruby walked out the front door of the warehouse. She sucked in a deep breath of air and focused on keeping her pace even on the sidewalk in case they were watching her leave. She scanned the adjoining streets, searching for the unmarked car that would undoubtedly be waiting for her, but it never came into view. With a confused frown, she turned the corner.

And ran smack into Troy.

He gripped her elbow, propelling her toward his black sedan parked at the curb. "Get in the goddamn car," he growled.

Ruby searched his face, which looked carved from stone, and decided protesting would only make things worse. "All right, fine," she responded, matching his tone. "Save the manhandling for later."

Troy pulled away from the curb mere seconds later, splitting his focus between the streets he navigated and the rearview mirror. For endless blocks, he appeared too angry to speak, but finally broke the silence. "Do you have a death wish, Ruby?"

She ignored his question. "Driscol is inside that warehouse. I confirmed it." He didn't say anything in response, just stared straight ahead, jaw grinding together. When they'd driven at least twenty blocks, he pulled into an empty lot running alongside a park. Still, he didn't turn to look at her. "I know you're angry, but look at me, I'm fine." She unhooked her seat belt and faced him. "Aren't you going to call someone about this? Lenny is in there. I just spoke with him."

"Why would you do this?" Troy asked quietly. His tone began to alarm Ruby. Why wouldn't he look at her? "God, I knew you were hiding something, but this…" He shook his head. "This is foolish even by your standards."

"Foolish?" She laughed without humor, shock at his harsh words trickling through her chest. "Did you know he was there? Did you know he's been coming and going through the parking garage behind the building? Or that, including Lenny, there are eight armed men inside?" His grip on the steering wheel tightened and his knuckles went white, but he didn't respond. "No, I don't think you did. I was trying to help. And I *did*."

When he finally looked at her, she paled at his haunted expression. "I didn't ask for your help. I never *wanted* or *needed* your brand of help."

"You didn't have to ask." She swallowed the lump in her throat, despising the tears that threatened behind her eyelids. "That's the thing about me. Once I decide I'm in your corner, I'm hard to get rid of."

He leaned toward her, punctuating each word. "People in my corner die, Ruby. They *die*."

"That's bullshit," she choked out, alarmed by his eerie reaction. "If you insist on blaming yourself for Grant's death, I can't stop you. But the situations don't compare. I did this to *avoid* you ending up like Grant. I wanted you to be prepared."

"Go ahead and justify it to yourself. It doesn't change the fact that you lied to me, or that you deliberately chose to place yourself in danger rather than actually trust me for one goddamn minute." He made a bitter noise. "It's like I'm a fucking magnet for reckless head cases looking to get their rocks off."

Pain blooming in her chest, she laughed shakily. "Well, you can't say I didn't warn you." Her comment went unappreciated by Troy, so she tried again. "I was worried. I know what he's capable of, and I didn't want to lose you…or see you hurt."

He punched the steering wheel. "Do you think it would have been somehow easier for me to lose *you,* since I'm so used to loss? At this point, what's one more death on my head, right?" His voice vibrated with emotion. "The situation *is* the same. I don't know how… We've known each other less than a week. But if something had happened today, Ruby, it would have fucked me up just as much as Grant's death. Maybe…more. So if it's too soon for you to feel the same, too bad. You're important to me. And you could have already been gone."

Ruby's chest rose and fell rapidly as she absorbed his unexpected words. She didn't know how to respond. Deeds not words. It was all she knew. She wouldn't have gone through with her plan today unless she felt something significant for him. Why couldn't he see that? She didn't know how to express it any other way. "You're important to me, too," she whispered, silently begging Troy to understand what he meant to her, but he only stared quietly out the car window.

They sat there in silence for long, torturous minutes but neither of them spoke again. Anger, resentment, and something akin to defeat radiated from Troy in the driver's seat. She jumped when he turned the key in the ignition and started the car.

"Where are we going?" she asked huskily as they pulled out of the parking lot.

"I'm taking you home."

Panic spread through her at the finality in his voice. "Are you coming with me?"

"No." He shook his head. "We can't do this anymore, Ruby."

Her heart beat loudly in her ears, drowning out the car's engine. "Do what?" Troy didn't answer. "Look at me!"

His eyes slid shut for a moment before he faced her. Even then, he appeared to be looking straight through her where she sat in the passenger seat. "You were in danger before just by associating with me. Now? I'm a complete liability to you." His throat worked with emotion. "Not to mention, there will inevitably be more cases like this involving people from your past. I can't risk you doing this kind of thing again. I can't risk you at all."

She shook her head as if to clear it. "You're cutting me loose to keep me safe. Is that what you're saying? That's crazy."

"I don't know how else to do it. I asked you for one simple thing, to trust me, to let me keep you safe, and you couldn't give it to me."

"You think trust is *easy* for me?"

"No. I don't." He rolled one shoulder. "In fact, maybe it's impossible."

Ruby stared out the front windshield, cars and trees blurring together as they passed. On the right, her building came into view over the Chinese take-out restaurant. Only this morning, she'd woken with Troy in her bed. Happiness had wormed its way inside her, but now it threatened to detonate like a ticking time bomb. Her chest constricted at the thought of him dropping her off and leaving, but at that moment, she couldn't think of a single thing to convince him to stay.

When he spoke, his voice was devoid of emotion. "You need to stay home until we make an arrest. I asked to have a new officer assigned to you, since the other one obviously can't do his job. He's in the car behind me. Ruby, if you leave the house, he has orders to arrest you." He didn't react to her incredulous expression. "If that's the only way to keep you from jeopardizing yourself, so be it. You interfered with an investigation this afternoon. The choice is no longer mine."

Ruby absorbed his callously delivered words, then nodded tightly. Intent on hiding the pain curling through her system determined to buckle her, she straightened her spine and placed one hand on the door handle. "If you leave me right now, it will be the last time we're together. Don't ever come back. I won't give you the time of day." She met his stormy gaze. "That's a promise. And I never break a promise."

She gave him five long, painful seconds to respond, but besides a muscle working in his jaw and the accelerated rise and fall of his chest, he showed no reaction.

Ruby got out of the car and closed the door behind her. She refused to turn around and show him the tears streaming down her cheeks. Would never give anyone the satisfaction of seeing her cry. If he'd truly wanted to hurt her, he'd succeeded with flying colors. It felt as though her heart was trying to claw its way out of her chest.

As she reached the door, keys in hand, she saw it stood slightly ajar. She hesitated for a moment with her hand on the knob, debating whether or not she should go in. Occasionally, the restaurant workers from downstairs used the stairwell to smoke, especially in winter. Today, however, she felt a little jumpy. Then she heard a faint groan of pain and recognized it right away from her memories. Bowen. Without another thought, save the fact that her friend was in pain, she pulled open the door and went inside.

Bowen lay in the far corner, writhing on the floor and holding his ribs, his face covered in blood. He looked up at her, apology in his half-swelled-shut eye. "I'm sorry, Ruby, I tried to stop them."

The door slammed, and two sets of hands grabbed her from behind.

Chapter Twelve

Troy sat in his idling car, watching Ruby walk toward her building. Every step she took in the opposite direction filled him with more and more panic. *Don't ever come back*. His instincts were demanding that he go to her, carry her up the stairs, and hold her until the sickening fear passed. If it ever did. No amount of time would erase the dread he'd felt racing into Brooklyn, knowing once he got there his team would go in guns blazing, Ruby helpless in the crossfire. When they'd pulled up as she'd exited, he'd been staggered by relief, but the emotion had fast been replaced by fury. Fury over Ruby putting herself in such a vulnerable position. Fury over her secretiveness.

Fury at himself for not seeing what she had planned.

It felt so incredibly familiar. He'd experienced it before, the split second of fear where he realized the person he would die for without hesitation hadn't even given him the damn chance. Only this time, the split second had stretched into an intolerable fifteen minutes where he'd been unable to see anything but Ruby amid a sea of gunfire. His worst fear realized.

He had to believe this was the right thing to do. The farther she stayed from him, the safer she would be. She might have managed to distance herself from her past, but in the space of a single afternoon, she'd ingratiated herself with the same crowd. On his behalf. If she'd never met him, if he hadn't pursued her with such single-mindedness, today wouldn't have happened. Their relationship could have easily been responsible for her death today.

As she pulled the door open to her building and disappeared from his view, Troy felt it slam behind her like a physical blow. She hadn't even looked back once. Already he missed the very sight of her. Her scent lingered in the car, taunting him, reminding him of the fierce pleasure he'd derived from smelling her on his pillow. In his bed.

Jesus. This feels like a mistake.

His phone vibrated in his pocket, giving him a much-needed distraction.

"Bennett," he answered, his voice raw.

"Hey," Daniel's voice rang in his ear. "Everything all right?"

"Fuck no."

"Yeah, it doesn't sound like it."

Troy pinched the bridge of his nose. "Let Rhodes know to hold off on the raid. We were right. There's a back entrance into location number two through the parking garage. Driscol is inside with eight armed men."

Daniel laughed incredulously. "That's why she went in there, isn't it? To scope the place out. Jesus, you've got your hands full with that one. Rhodes is going to want to talk to her."

"No shit. I'm putting it off as long as I can." He put the car into drive. "Let him know I placed new protection on her. I'm heading back in."

It took Troy a full minute to actually pull away from the curb, his urge to go inside after Ruby so incredibly strong that he didn't think he could drive away. He coasted to a stop at the first red light at the end of her block, idling with his foot firmly on the break. The light turned green, and still he didn't move.

She would be safer this way, he reminded himself. She'd survived incredible odds without him for years. Then he'd walked into her life and, within a week, she was taking life-threatening risks. He couldn't let it happen again. That afternoon he brought her home from school, when she'd revealed her association to Driscol…he should have walked away then. This was his punishment. Knowing what it was like to sleep with her in his arms and having to give her up.

Still, Troy couldn't go. He physically couldn't bring himself to drive any farther from her.

The memory of Ruby walking into her building and slamming the door behind her played on a loop in his mind, over and over until he felt a familiar sense of trepidation creeping up his spine. Struck by a sudden thought, he glanced at the rearview mirror, back toward Ruby's building. Something was bothering him, and he couldn't shake it. When it finally hit him, Troy sprang into action. He quickly pressed the distress button on his police radio, flung open his door, and started running.

She hadn't used her keys. Before she'd walked into the building, she'd reached into her pocket and took out her keys, but she hadn't used them.

· · ·

Ruby tried to twist around to see the men who'd grabbed her, but as they dragged her up the stairs, her knees slammed painfully into each step. Her jeans ripped, the metal scraping her knees raw. She opened her mouth to scream, but a clammy palm slapped over her mouth.

Lenny Driscol stood at the top of the stairs.

At once, she felt numb. The men dragging her were making no effort to keep her uninjured, and that told her exactly what was coming. She let her body go limp, emotional and physical pain blurring together until she couldn't feel a thing.

All for nothing. She'd done it all for nothing. How many times in her life had she been told by her father or men she hustled that her reckless arrogance would be her downfall? That someday it would take a giant bite out of her ass? She'd laughed in their faces, but they'd been right. Today, she'd done the same thing she always did, putting herself at risk without thinking of the consequences, and now she would pay. Twice. After all, she'd lost the man, too. A man she'd fallen for. All for *nothing*.

They reached the top of the stairs. She forced herself to stand and limp into the apartment, but her legs gave out, and she ended up crawling over the door frame on her bloody knees, past a smiling Lenny. Humiliation burned her from the inside, followed by outrage when she saw two of her custom pool cues had been snapped in half. She grabbed the back of a chair and pulled herself into it, holding in a whimper of relief.

As the men disappeared back down the stairs, she looked up at Lenny defiantly, refusing to waver in her cool appraisal of him. "Make yourself at home," she said with an indifferent shrug.

Lenny laughed, but she could sense his underlying irritation. "I wonder what it would take to get you off your high horse." His smile widened. "I shouldn't have to wonder much longer."

The two men reappeared in her doorway, tossing a half-unconscious Bowen at her feet. Lenny watched her closely, waiting for a reaction, but she managed to keep the disgust and horror off her face. If he'd do this to his own son, what would he do to her? When Lenny turned to close her apartment door, she glimpsed the gun at the small of his back. With a nervous swallow, she risked a look down at Bowen and couldn't stop herself from flinching. Another person she'd hurt with her thoughtless behavior. Perhaps she deserved whatever she got.

"You must think I'm pretty stupid, Ruby," Lenny said, circling her chair. "You decide to go straight, drop off the radar for a year, and then reappear, looking for a game." He stopped in front of her, leaned down near her face. "And if that didn't tip me off that you were trying to screw me, the unmarked car that dropped you off outside would have. The second you left the warehouse, I got the hell out of there because I knew a raid was coming. I was right." He shrugged. "I should thank you *and* my son for tipping me off. You were barely out the door before he slipped away to warn you I was coming."

"Dammit, Bowie," she whispered shakily, then glared in Lenny's direction. Humiliation mixed with grief. She'd likely blown the arrest and gotten Bowen hurt in the process. If she'd stayed out of it, none of this would be happening. Instead, she'd gone and jeopardized Troy, Bowen, and herself when she'd intended on the exact opposite. Her throat tightened, emotions threatening to give way. "I guess monsters are born, not made. Thank God Bowen is nothing like you."

Lenny's eyes glittered dangerously. He stepped away from her, rubbing the back of his neck with jerky movements. Then he took a giant step forward and slapped her across the face, hard enough to knock her off the chair. Stinging pain radiated from her cheek; a surprised cry tore from her lips. Bowen stirred on the floor beside her, attempting to shield her, but she put a hand on his cheek and told him to stay down. She didn't think she could endure watching him be punished any more for her mistake.

A hand circled her neck and yanked her off the floor. She was thrown back into the chair, choking and dragging in deep gulps of air. Helplessly, she watched as Lenny reached into the back of his jeans for his gun.

This is it. This is it, her mind repeated continuously until she started saying it out loud as well. Ruby squeezed her eyes shut, not wanting the final image she ever saw to be Lenny's face.

Her apartment door crashed open, followed by the unmistakable cocking of a gun and a voice that sent relief racing through her body.

"I wouldn't reach for that gun, Mr. Driscol." Troy's voice vibrated with intensity. Both of Lenny's men reach into their jackets. "You two, either. My backup just arrived. You won't make it out of the building."

Several other police officers entered the apartment behind Troy, guns drawn. With rapid efficiency, they divested Lenny's men of their weapons and handcuffed them. Troy didn't take his gun off Lenny until the other threats had been removed, but then he confiscated the gun from Lenny's waistband and pushed him down to handcuff him. For the first time since he'd entered the apartment, Ruby could see Troy.

As he placed the handcuffs on a resigned Lenny, Troy's gaze ran over her anxiously, teeth clenching when he saw her ruined knees. Two officers she recognized from Quincy's stepped in to take over handcuffing Lenny, as if anticipating what he might do. Remorse, apology, anger, and need warred on his face as he watched her. But so many emotions warred inside her that she couldn't stand the weight of his, too. It reminded her of what she'd done. How she'd risked him. Risked what they might have had together. And she hated seeing his remorse because she didn't deserve it.

"Tell me you're okay," he demanded when he'd gotten himself under control.

With a shaky nod, Ruby tore her gaze away from him and focused on something she could do to help repair the damage. She dropped off the chair onto the floor, ignoring the pain it caused her knees, and used the edge of her coat to wipe blood from Bowen's face. He shrugged her off, moving with difficulty into a sitting position. She looked up at the room in general. "Can someone please call an ambulance?"

She felt Troy behind her. "It's already on the way." He knelt down next to her, but she ignored him, couldn't stand to see sympathy in his eyes. She felt him slide an arm around her waist, and barely resisted the urge to lean into his warmth. "Sit back up on the chair, baby. Your knees..." He cleared his throat. "You need the ambulance, too."

"No. I'm fine."

"You're not fine," he grated. "Neither of us are fine."

As if on cue, three paramedics filed into the apartment and went straight for Bowen, who finally spoke up. "I'm good here, Rube," he said, expression thoughtful as he watched Troy. "Go get yourself patched up."

Troy stood over her while the paramedic cut her jeans to the knee so he could clean and bandage her wounds. She could practically feel the tension rolling off Troy, but her own mental strain easily matched his. More than anything, she wanted everyone out of her apartment so she could bury her face in a pillow and cry. She hadn't cried since her father left to go back out on the road a year prior. Now it felt like tiny cracks were forming in her exterior, ready to burst.

Lenny and his men were escorted down the stairs and placed in the backs of separate patrol cars. All three of them complained over their rough treatment and yelled for lawyers as they went. Bowen's injuries required further medical treatment, and although he protested vehemently, they finally convinced him if he didn't get stitches, his face might not heal correctly. That got him moving.

Finally, she and Troy were left alone in the apartment. He closed the door behind the final officer and turned to face her. When he started to speak, she cut him off.

"I already know what you're going to say, so please… Save your breath."

"You have no clue what I'm going to say."

Ruby raised her head to find his gaze riveted on her, drawing her in. She quickly looked away. "Sure, I do. I put myself and others in danger, including you. I acted foolishly. I need to stay away from you for my own good, as well as yours." She gave a single, shaky nod. "Finally, we agree on something. You were right to leave. You should get as far away from me as possible."

Troy went very still, unease moving across his face. "Ruby—"

"Just leave me. Please."

"Don't ask me to do that," he said, coming toward her. "We both made mistakes today, but right now, in this moment, we need each other. Don't let pride get in the way of that."

"This isn't about pride." She hated the defeat in her voice, but the numbness wouldn't let anything else through. Maybe her refusal *was* based on pride. In the last hour, hers had taken a tremendous hit. She felt exposed, embarrassed… Everything she'd ever stood for had been thrown in her face. But right now, she didn't care about the reason, only knew she wanted him to leave her in peace so she could scrape up the broken pieces. "Go home, Troy. You caught the bad guy and saved the reckless head case from certain death. It's over."

Troy knelt down in front of her, his voice vibrating with emotion. "No, it's not. But nothing I say right now is going to get through, is it?" She didn't answer, just stared down at him while doing her best to keep a blank expression. He cupped her ankles and slid his warm hands slowly up to the backs of her knees, his touch so achingly tender that her entire body shook uncontrollably. After the emotional upheaval of the last hour, his touch felt like a healing balm even as it demolished her. Troy leaned forward and pressed light kisses to the bandages on her knees, apologizing between each kiss. "I'm so sorry, Ruby. So sorry."

Her throat clogged with the sobs dying to break free. He wasn't going to leave. She could see it on his face, in the fierceness of his expression. Her hands ached to reach out and trace his furrowed brow. Feel the scrape of his beard against her cheek. But another, equally potent part of her could only see her shortcomings when she looked at his face right now. She would have to *make* him leave. Her composure was starting to slip past the point of no return. "I told you if you left, it would be the last time we were together," she whispered and watched his face cloud. "I never break a promise, Troy. Get *out*."

Before he left, he paused at the door. "They're going to need you to come in to make a statement. I want to take you in myself, but if you'd rather someone el—"

"I would."

He nodded once. When he walked out the door a moment later, one of the officers she recognized came in, introduced himself as Brent, and drove her down to the station. She saw Troy through a glass partition when she arrived, but ignored him as she was led to an interrogation room. Thankfully, Brent ended up taking her statement. He hadn't forced her to talk on the ride into Manhattan and didn't keep her there longer than needed, which she appreciated. As he jotted down her monotone answers on a legal pad, her detailed account of events and her reasons behind them sounded ill-advised to her own ears, sinking her even deeper into the black pit she'd descended into.

Brent offered to give her a ride back to Brooklyn, but she declined, wanting desperately to get away from anything reminding her of Troy or the events of the afternoon. When she arrived home half an hour later, it felt like a dam breaking. She slammed her apartment door, limped to her bed, lay down, and didn't get up for a very long time.

Chapter Thirteen

Troy's vision blurred as he poured his fifth tumbler of whiskey. He couldn't recall how much time had passed since he'd walked through the door and fallen into the dining room chair. It could have been seconds, hours, days. There was an image seared into his brain he couldn't shake. His loose objective had been to drink until it faded from his memory, but the more liquor he consumed, the more he thought of Ruby, cut and bleeding, staring her own death in the face. If he'd been one second later...just one second...

He raised the glass to his lips and took a long pull, welcoming the burn in his chest as the liquid went through him. The image alone would have been enough to give him nightmares for the rest of his life, but her defeated attitude afterward made it infinitely worse. She'd never been defeated a day in her life. He would lay every cent he had on it. He'd done that to her. Given her nothing to hold on to. No reason to fight. He'd driven away, leaving her to battle a homicidal criminal on her own. He would never forgive himself. Never.

Troy pushed back his chair and stood. He paced the

kitchen, mind racing from one thought to the next. Was she asleep, battling the same nightmares he was avoiding? Was she in pain? The thought made him crazy. Made him ache as if the injuries were his own, instead of Ruby's.

He desperately needed a distraction or he would lose what little sanity he had left. Today had been hell for more than one reason. Snatching his phone off the table, he knew he couldn't put off the call he'd been dreading since this morning off any longer. He blew out a deep breath and pressed a number he'd had on speed dial for years. Judith, Grant's widow, answered on the third ring.

"Hello?" Judith's voice, along with a duo of children's voices in the background. It sounded so familiar it gave him momentary pause. "Hello?"

"Judith, its Troy."

"Troy," she greeted him warmly. "I had a feeling you'd call today."

He sat back down in the dining room chair. "I should have called earlier. It's been a hectic day."

She laughed under her breath. "I remember those too well."

Of course she would. "How are you?"

"Oh, you know...coping. Grant would have been thirty today." She sighed. "It would have been one hell of a party."

Troy smiled. "If I recall correctly, for this twenty-eighth, he insisted on setting up the kids' Slip'N Slide on the front lawn."

"Yeah. At *2:00 a.m.* The neighbors were thrilled." They both laughed. "So how has New York been so far?"

Just like that, his stubborn thoughts went back to Ruby. Guilt assailed him. His best friend's widow was on the other line and he couldn't get Ruby out of his head.

"Uh-oh. Radio silence is never a good sign. What's her name, stud?"

"Judith, we really don't—"

"Please," she implored, her tone suddenly serious. "Take my mind off things for a few minutes Troy. I'd appreciate it."

Troy massaged his forehead where a dull throbbing had formed. "Ruby. Her name is Ruby. She's a professional pool hustler with an attitude the size of fucking Illinois. She's a spectacular pain in the ass." He leaned back in his chair, releasing a slow breath. "She's also beautiful, brave, and loyal. And way too smart for her own good."

"Damn. What the hell are you wasting your time talking to me for?" Judith laughed. "A professional pool hustler, huh? I bet you're just tickled over that safe, boring career choice."

"Was it obvious?"

"Huh." Judith stayed silent a moment. Troy could practically hear her drawing her own conclusions. "You know, we never really talked about the night Grant…you know," she started hesitantly. "I don't think I'm even ready now. But Troy? We both know nothing you said or did could have stopped him from swooping in and trying to be the hero. I married a cowboy. I knew it from the beginning." A beat passed. "And I loved him *for* it, not in spite of it."

Her words dropped like tiny bombshells onto Troy's head, cutting straight through the fog brought on by the alcohol he'd consumed. "Judith—"

"I have to go. The kids…" Judith trailed off. He sensed the conversation had been too much for her, so he said good-bye and hung up, her words ringing in his head. He'd never expected or even wanted for her to absolve him of Grant's death, but he couldn't deny feeling a sense of peace for the first time in months. He didn't feel better, that would take much longer, but he felt slightly lighter than before.

I loved him for *it, not in spite of it.*

Troy stood and looked out the window toward Brooklyn. He'd known from the second Ruby walked into Quincy's that there was nothing *safe* about her. It hadn't stopped him, though. He'd gone after her like a man obsessed, incapable of making any other choice but the one that kept her in his arms. She'd excited him, challenged him, and made him human again after he'd spent so much time shutting out anything that made him feel.

Troy's head dropped forward as if a cord holding it upright had been cut, a sickening pit forming in his stomach as he remembered her dejected face as she'd gotten out of his car. After he'd told her he couldn't be with her. Jesus, he'd fallen hard for a girl with abandonment issues, and he'd already proven to her that he was no different than anyone who'd done the same in the past. A *stubborn-as-hell* girl who'd promised she would never again give him the time of day.

He'd well and truly screwed up this time. Too bad he could be just as stubborn and determined as Ruby when he wanted something. In no world did there exist the possibility where he accepted her decision and let her walk. As of right now, he only had one advantage working in his favor.

She'd fallen for him, too.

If he hadn't been blinded by his fear of losing her, he'd have realized her risky stunt today had been Ruby's unique way of telling him. Tomorrow he would need to remind her why.

• • •

Ruby woke the next morning with a gasp after a twelve solid hours of sleep. As if her brain had shut off out of necessity, she'd slept in a black, dreamless void. Now, however, the events of the day before rushed back in a blast of clarity, catapulting her back down onto her pillow. Troy's parting words floated over her, slaying her all over again. He'd been on his knees, kissing her and apologizing. So she'd thrown him out. Did that make her insane or stupid?

Twice in her life she'd felt the sting of abandonment. First, with her father and yesterday with Troy. She'd opened herself up for a wealth of pain, and she'd been rewarded in spades for letting her guard down. He said he'd left for her own good, but he'd broken her heart in the process, and for the first time since she could remember, she'd felt robbed of her usual inner strength. When she'd sat in the chair, waiting for Lenny to pull his gun, a tiny part of her had been too tired to fight. That kind of mentality was dangerous for someone like her. She'd always been a survivor, and in the space of five minutes, Troy's leaving had robbed her of that. She couldn't forgive him for it, nor could she forgive herself.

Every dull beat of her heart echoed in her ears as if it had literally been damaged. It hurt to think or move or breathe. She could fix herself by going to him, apologizing for her rash actions, and forgiving him for leaving. He'd take away all the pain. Until the next time. There would always be a next time.

After testing her knees by bending them toward her stomach, she swung her legs over the side of the bed and went to shower. Not wanting any reminder of yesterday, she ripped off the bandages and threw them in the trash. She drew strength from the hot water rushing over her damaged skin, the sting helping to fight the numbness. This wouldn't beat her. She had too many plans and had come too far. Yesterday, she'd been broken, so today, she would begin to fix herself. Sort through the ashes and build on whatever parts of her had survived. Adding new parts as she went. Brazening it out as usual.

Ruby had a lot of experience blocking painful thoughts. It hurt to think of Troy, so she simply wouldn't. Perhaps right now, when everything remained so fresh, the feat proved impossible. But over time, she would do it. She would forget the man who'd stormed into her life, commanded the possession of her body, her heart. After all, she didn't have any other option, did she?

Knowing how important it was to make her 9:00 a.m. class, she tugged on her jeans and jammed her feet into her leather boots. Her pool stick sat in the corner, catching her eye, but she didn't grab it and sling it over her shoulder as she normally would. At the bottom of the stairs, she pushed open the door and came to a dead stop.

Troy leaned against his car, arms crossed, clearly waiting for her. He looked terrible, eyes red-rimmed, hair sticking up in every direction. When he saw her exit, he pushed off his car and took a step toward her. Without thinking, Ruby backed up. Otherwise, she would have run at him full-force and thrown herself at him. That would never work. She teetered right on the edge, and if he touched her, she would fall, hands flailing, into the ravine.

"What are you doing here?" she asked, grateful to hear she didn't sound half as pathetic as she felt. "I told you it's over."

"The hell it is." He responded immediately, his face rife with determination. "We both made mistakes yesterday, but I'll be damned before I let us walk away from this." Coming closer, his head shook slowly. "We don't end here. I know that because I won't *allow* it."

"You're the one who walked." As soon as the words left her mouth, she wanted to take them back. She didn't want him to know how much he'd hurt her. Didn't *want* to hurt this much. If she talked about it, the pain would only worsen. "Look, I don't have time for this. I have a class." She started to walk toward the subway entrance, but his words stopped her.

"I didn't make it one goddamn block yesterday, Ruby." He swiped an impatient hand through his hair. "Look, we're both stubborn hotheads, and we're going to fight. Early and often. But I will *never* make it more than one block before

I come back. That is my *promise* to you. And I don't break my promises, either." Hands on hips, he breathed deeply as if attempting to calm himself. "If I let my fear of losing you keep us apart, I get the same damn result. The only way I can fight that fear is if you fight it with me."

His raw honestly toppled her defenses. "I don't have any fight in me right now, Troy," she murmured before she thought better of it.

"Yes, you do." He reached out and cupped her cheeks. "You've got more fight than anyone I know. I'm sorry I made you think otherwise for even a second."

Ruby pulled away, moving once again in the direction of subway. "I'm sorry, too. But I can't do this."

"I'm going to come back tomorrow," he called after her. "And the day after that. Every single day, I'll come for you. As long as it takes, Ruby. I'm not giving you up."

· · ·

True to his word, Troy came back every single morning for a week. Ruby woke up each day and looked out her living room window to find him leaning against his car, arms crossed, waiting for her in the cold. After that first morning, they didn't speak to each other. They didn't need to. Everything she needed to know communicated itself through Troy's eyes. With a single glance, he told her he wasn't going anywhere. He would be back, day after day, to torment her.

Some mornings, he looked her over impatiently, as though he wanted to throw her over his shoulder and carry her back upstairs. Those were the times Ruby found it hardest to keep walking. Her need for him grew stronger by the day, and she sensed he knew it. He started calling her on the phone, waking her up in bed. Once, when she finally answered against her better judgment, he'd rasped, "Let me in, baby. Now."

She'd been forced to take a cold shower before leaving the apartment for class that day.

As the week wore on, his presence started to comfort her. She stopped seeing her mistake and the subsequent pain he'd wrought every time she looked at him. Instead, she started looking forward to the mornings, when she could memorize his image and carry it with her all day. She started to believe in what he'd said, that he wouldn't allow them to end. That he would come back every day until she realized it.

One thing, she already knew for certain. Her plan to get over him had died in its earliest stages. As long as he kept showing up, looking sexy, sleep deprived, and determined, her feelings for him would only continue to intensify. This was the man who'd tracked her down at school and brought her home. Held her tightly while she slept as though she might vanish. She didn't want to punish him any longer. His reasons for walking away hadn't been selfish, but that's precisely how she was acting. Selfish. Punishing him—and herself in the process.

Not anymore, Ruby decided as she sprung out of bed that morning, feeling more like herself than she had in days. After throwing on her robe, she padded toward the window with a smile on her face, anxious to get her first look at Troy.

He wasn't there.

Ruby's stomach dropped to the floor. She pulled up the window and leaned out, looking for his car down the block, but it was nowhere in sight. With shaky hands, she closed the window and stood very still in the dim apartment. The first thought to pop into her head was, *Oh, God. I waited too long.*

Her second thought? *Screw that.*

She pulled her cell phone out of the charger and dialed Troy's number while pacing in front of the window. He answered on the first ring. "Hey, I'm—"

"One week? One week was your limit? You said *as long as it takes*, so where are you?" She swallowed around the tightness in her throat. "You said I was *your* pain in the ass. Well, get your ass over here so I can be a pain in it. Maybe you gave up after one week, but I haven't. I miss you, okay? I miss you, and you're supposed to be outside."

"*Ruby*," he broke in. "Look out your window." She spun around in time to see him pull up at the curb and get out of his car, still holding the phone to his ear. "I just hit a little traffic."

"Oh," she managed lamely. Before she could ponder the intelligence of going outside in freezing weather wearing a thin robe and no shoes, she dropped the phone and flung open her apartment door. She ran down the stairs and out of the building. Troy stood on the other side of the door when she pulled it open, devouring the sight of her before she jumped into his arms.

"Christ, I missed you, t—"

Her mouth cut him off. She wrapped her legs around his waist and kissed him, pouring everything she had into it. He returned the kiss with a tortured groan as he backed her into the building hallway and began ascending the stairs with her clinging to his tall frame. They didn't come up for air until they were inside her apartment and Troy kicked the door shut behind them.

"Maybe I should have hit traffic sooner," he mumbled against her mouth, making her laugh.

Desperate for the feel of his skin, she slipped down his body and immediately began removing his clothes. She peeled off his jacket and shirt as their mouths slanted over each other's greedily. Her anxious fingers worked his belt buckle, a moan passing through her lips when she felt the thick ridge behind his fly. When she paused to brush her palm over it, Troy's head fell forward against the door above her shoulder.

"God, please touch it. It hurts so bad," he growled, freeing himself from his pants. "I've been going mad every morning, knowing you were up here all naked and soft. I've got to have you now, baby. Let me have you or I'm going to lose my mind. I can't think. I can't *think*."

Ruby let her robe drop to the ground, and within seconds, he'd levered her against the door and thrust deep, their groans of relief colliding between them.

"I thought you gave up," she said unsteadily, her mouth moving on his bare shoulder.

Troy went still, forcing her to look him in the eye. What she saw there made her heart pound loudly in her chest. He kissed her lips softly, then turned and walked them toward her bedroom. He laid her on the rumpled sheets and came down on top of her, propping himself on his elbows. "I would have stood out there waiting forever. Don't ever doubt that." He pushed his hips forward, and Ruby gasped. "You're going to give me sleepless nights, Ruby, and I'm signing on for it. I'll have way more sleepless nights without you." He leaned down and kissed her neck, started to move. "We'll argue, and then we'll make up. And every time, we'll be stronger for it." His intense expression softened. "It's simple. You're for me, Ruby."

"I'm for you," she breathed.

Troy smiled, took her hands, and held them over her head as his rhythm increased. "Now. We're going to stay in this bed until I get tired of hearing you say you're mine. It's the only thing allowed out of your mouth for the next several hours. Is that clear?"

Eyes fluttering closed, she nodded. "Yes."

He nipped her bottom lip. "Follow the rules."

"I'm yours, Troy. I'm yours. *Yours*."

Acknowledgments

To everyone who bought my first book, *Protecting What's His*, thank you for all the encouraging comments and requests for more of my work. I didn't expect such a warm reception and I can't express how much I appreciate it.

To my husband, Patrick, who understands every time we need to pause a movie indefinitely so I can rush to my laptop and begin a new pass of edits.

To Heather Howland, who never stops working or plotting. I'm so lucky to work with you!

About the Author

New York Times and *USA TODAY* bestselling author Tessa Bailey lives in Brooklyn, New York, with her husband and young daughter. When she isn't writing or reading romance, she enjoys a good argument and thirty-minute recipes.

www.tessabailey.com

Join Bailey's Babes!

Discover more Entangled Select Suspense titles...

Burnout
an *NYPD Blue & Gold* novel by Tee O'Fallon

Sexy-as-sin Police Chief Mike Flannery knows the new arrival to Hopewell Springs is trouble; he's been a cop too long not to recognize the signs of a woman running from her past. But he can't resist her quick wit, smoking-hot body, and the easy way she embraces their close-knit community. NYPD Detective Cassie Yates is on the run. Armed with fake ID, her K-9, and a police-issued SUV, she flees to this quiet upstate town to avoid a hit. When the hired assassin hunts her down, Mike's past comes roaring back and secrets are revealed in an explosion destined to tear them apart—if not destroy them.

On Her Six
an *Under Covers* novel by Christina Elle

New neighbors are bad news in Samantha Harper's experience. Especially ones as suspicious and brooding as the guy who just moved in next door. So when the dangerous but sexy stranger seems to be involved in something illegal—the aspiring cop in her takes action. All DEA agent Ash Cooper wants to do is lay low and survive this crap surveillance assignment. But after a run-in with his attractive neighbor, he realizes that's going to be much harder than he planned. Keeping the woman out of trouble is hard enough, but keeping his hands off her is near impossible.

Printed in the USA
CPSIA information can be obtained
at www.ICGtesting.com
LVHW050819091123
763265LV00066B/2169

9 781682 812419